# 사랑, 그 빛을 찾아

# 사랑, 그 빛을 찾아

ⓒ 이미자, 2023

초판 1쇄 발행 2023년 11월 24일

지은이    이미자
펴낸이    이기봉
편집      좋은땅 편집팀
펴낸곳    도서출판 좋은땅
주소      서울특별시 마포구 양화로12길 26 지월드빌딩 (서교동 395-7)
전화      02)374-8616~7
팩스      02)374-8614
이메일    gworldbook@naver.com
홈페이지  www.g-world.co.kr

ISBN    979-11-388-2518-4 (03810)

# 사랑,

## 그 빛을 찾아

자유의
빛에 취하여

이미자 지음

좋은땅

# 차례

제1부

무상(無常)

# 소리

그대,
서러운 마음에 서러운 몸속 깊숙이에도
이율배반인 삶의 소리에
그대는 아침에 눈 떠 저녁에
그 소리가 춤추는 벽 앞에 드러눕는다
수많은 지껄임 속에
외로이 고달픈 소리 하나에
또 하나
눈물일랑, 웃음일랑
애조 띤 가락 속으로 숨어들어
떠돌며 미친 듯 춤추는 생명의 소리
그대는 몸속에 풀잎을 키우고
바람에 날리운 채
강물에 씻기운 채
그 몸속 깊숙이 자리 잡은 소리를 따라 살어
그 우울, 그 고독, 그 눈길,
그 육체의 눈빛 속,
깊숙한 곳에 자리 잡은 자유를 찾아가야지

그 모든 소리에의 유희
그 유희 속에 잠긴 생의 모든 것
그리고 내 안의 소리……

# 산

늘, 그렇게 산처럼 닿아 서서 산이 되어 버리자꾸나
들, 먼 데 들이 우는 소리
바다, 바다로 맨발로 달려들어 가 보렴

소리! 그대 살 속에서 소리가 난다
그대는 산이 되어 메아리 울리운다

그대는 더 이상 그 무엇을 구해서는 안 되리

홀로 들어앉은 者!

산이 되고

때론, 바다로 가서
거기서 그렇게 살자꾸나!

# 숲속

낙엽 뒤덮여,
우리의 수증기들
함께 핥는 고뇌,
이슬 머금은 풀잎 새
어린 산새들 수없이 애무하다
그리움을 추스르는데
먼 데
보이지 않는 가까운 나날들의 헐어 버린 애정의 걸음들

햇살은 좀 더
작은 짚 더미 위로,
햇살은 좀 더 은밀한 그늘 속,
깊숙한 둥지 위로,
만나기 위하여 깊은 산속
홀로 휘어지는 안개마냥
우리의 헐어 버린 애정의 걸음들 위로…

# 우리

오랫동안 우리는 슬퍼서 우리의 몸을 숨겼다
그늘 속에,
정적이 깔려 드는 햇살 속에,
우리의 눈물
바다에 가 하나의 꿈으로 화(化) 했던 그 지점에서
우리의 슬픔이 은빛 반짝이는 꿈을 춤추게 함을 보았다


우리의 혼(魂)이 스쳐 지나가던 물결 속에
우리의 혼(魂)이 하나의 파란 물결 속에서
더욱더 큰 물결로 일어나고 있었다


밤,
지금, 이 어두운 밤 속에
그들 물결이 격노하는 춤을 보아라
이곳에서 저곳으로
서로에게, 닿아 오며
만나기 위한 그들
설움의 양식을 보아라

# 거울

저 거울 속에는 벌거숭이인 나르시스가 서 있다
그렇게, 병(病)든 시간 속에 침묵하는 내가 서 있다
아니, 못 견디게 보고 싶은 이의 고독이 써 있다
끝내, 치유되어야 할 방황에는
황량한 사랑의 손길이 숨어 있었다
나르시스! 창백히 푸르른 그의 이마
그의 성숙해 버린 홀로에의 익숙함,
그 진리의 빛이 너무 밝아
그 우수에 싸인 영혼은 너무나 가벼웠다
그 천진하고도 우스꽝스런 몸짓 속에
성숙해진 이마가 소생하는 평화를 이야기한다
이제 그의 겨울에도 봄이 오는가 보다
그의 성전, 그의 제단……
하얗고 보라색으로, 노랗게 꽃이 피는 그의 계절,
그와 더불어 난 너무도 많은 계절을 살았다
그러나 이제, 눈물도 없어야겠다
봄, 이 봄에 우리는 웃으면서 이별을 고하자
웃으면서, 새로운 사랑의 눈부심을 깨닫도록 하자
이제는 여러 길 중에서 한 길만을 타고 가야 하는,
자욱이 모험과 도박이 깔린 현실을 향해 열려 있고프다
묵은 옷들을 벗어 버리고,
훨훨 가벼이 새로운 공기를 마시고 싶다

그리하여, 저 거울에는 뭉게뭉게 피어나는 분홍빛 흰 구름과
드맑은 하늘, 가이없는 바다가 넘실대도록
바다!
바다를 동경하는 집시 아이의 투명한 영혼처럼,
순진하게 무르익은 웃음이 솜털마냥 포근히 자리 잡도록
돛을 달고 떠나자
그렇게 집이 없어, 자신 속으로 파고들어간 여자,
그 집시 여자를 위해 무언의 발라드를 쳐 주렴
아니, 뜨거운 축배의 잔을 드높이 쳐들럼
철 모르는 어린아이처럼 두 손 가득히 꽃다발을 들고서
치맛자락 날리며, 강뚝 위를 거닐자
그 욕심 없는 영혼을 사랑하자
아, 봄에는,
봄에는 깊은 정적으로 흐트러져 난무하는 눈송이처럼,
겨울의 고통이 하얀 것이었음을 용감히 뇌까리자
시작과 종말이 한 직선상에 머무는
生을 향해 용감히 뛰어들자
그리하여, 거울 속에 있는 나를 보며,
사랑 속에 하나가 된 우리의 영혼이,
따스한 양지 녘에 움터 오는 생명이 되어,
가이없는 바다에, 저 푸른 하늘에 웃음을 선사하도록……

# 밤거리

오려무나
꽃향기 일어나는 바람 속에 누워
사람의 섬 그늘이 사라지는
이 거리
밤이 깊어지면
우리네 감출 길 없는 허기짐도 깊어지려니
한 줌 별빛 차가울수록
홀로 중얼거리는 눈빛
펼쳐지는 청색 창공 위로
파랑 나비 춤추는 환상의 그늘 속

그렇게 오려무나
풀어헤친 머리
은비늘 반짝이며
실오라기 살 속
무수한 물길 내뿜으며

우리네 섬 그늘은
녹색 숨결들 서러울 때
떠 있는 눈빛 속으로 깊게 가라앉으려니

오래 뒹굴고 싶었던 바람 속

이슬을 마시며……

# 고독

모든 길들은 바다와 들판의 창공으로 열려져 있다
마음이여!
헛되이 타인의 이해와 올바른 인정에 연연해하지 마라
그대가 치솟아 올라야 할 것은
그들의 두 손에도,
시끄러운 귀와 입놀림에서도 벗어나
저 멀리 광활한 창공이어라

禪心은 평화로이 풀을 뜯는 양들을 친애하네
쓸데없이 걸었던
그대의 거리와 도시의 얼굴들의
기형화된, 불구화된 生의 깊숙한 보배의 화음들
정녕,
그것은 그대의 어린 걸음이었을 뿐
허황되이 그 속되고 하찮은 소음 사이에서도 찾을 수 있다고 믿은,
외로운 마음의 기도였다

쓸쓸한 늦봄의 체취는
말라빠진 음향 사이에서
모든 것들의 우울한 버림에 대한
희미한 새벽에로의 걸음이어라

마음이여~
모든 길들로 열려 있는
바다와 들판의 창공으로
은은한 콧노래나 부르렴

# 심연(深淵)

## I

아름다움은
텅 빈 가슴속에서
풀잎 흐느끼는
그늘진 바람 속에서

정신은 율동의 반복 속에
무료함이 사라질 때에
거침없이 대항하다
잠드는 아름다운 육신으로

채 다 가라앉지 않은
공간 가득히 난무하는 언어
언어의 숲속

벌거벗은 육신의 빛

불꽃 튕기는
상념의 그림자 비치지 않는
생소한 집
생소한 해저(海底)의 눈물

언어의 눈물들

춤도 없이,
언어의 집이 없는 곳

처절하게 생소하듯
의아한 눈빛

풀잎도,
바람 비껴가는 고독도
그곳엔 없어라
그곳엔 없어라

II

숨기듯이
아무도 무관한
神도 그곳에 초대받지 않은
영원한 흐름이 없어도 영원 속에서
존재하는 이름으로
어떠한 언어라도 살 수 있으며
어떠한 언어라도 진정한 본체일 수 없어

우리는 새로운 언어를 풀어 준다
새로운 언어의 공간을 축배한다

고뇌의 끝에서
영원의 축대를 박고
새로운 삶의
그 삶 속으로 이르는 섬들의 고뇌는
단 하나의 본체를 기억한다

자유!
자유!

자유라는

견고한,
엄숙한,
사랑으로……

# 살아간다는 것은

살아간다는 것은
타인의 삶을 응시한다는 것이다
뼛가루만 남도록
아파한다는 것이다
메꿀 수 없는 빈 구석으로 빠져들어 간다는 것이다
살아간다는 것은 아무것도 아닌 굴레에서
영혼을 입는다는 것이다
흔들리는 나무에 깃든 넋의 속삭임을 간직한다는 것이다
살아간다는 것은
분명한 이름을 찾기 위하여
미로 위에서 걷고 있다는 것이다

## 성체(聖體)

그는
늘,
그 시간이면
성당,
맨 끝 좌석에 앉아 성체의 불꽃을
그저 하염없이 바라볼 뿐이었습니다

일체함으로
타오르는 비상(飛翔)을 꿈꾸며……

# 흔적(痕迹)

모든 것이 물거품이 될 것입니다
좀먹었던 그 모든 유희와 장식과 치레들이
거리에서, 거리에서
산과 도시가 잇닿은 돌 구릉지 위에서
어차피의 존재는 그 도시 속에 파묻힌 생명이옵기에
조직화되어
더 이상의 인간이기를 침해하는
모순에 모순을 낳는 어지러운 회전

나의 존재함을 붙들었을 때
너의 존재가 비추어 주고 있음을
나의 빛은 너로 인하여 바라볼 수 있다는 걸
나의 가슴팍에 너의 얼굴을 묻고
울고 있는 너의 고통이 내 심장을 격동 치게 할 때
우리는 모두 한 줌 맑은 날의 이슬이어라

바위 위로 휘몰아치는
거센 파도
잠잠해질 사이
또다시 풍랑 속에 빠트리고,

우리는 하나의 빛을 이룬다

우리는 하나의 빛을 이룬다

# 수레바퀴

산 위에서
구릉지 아래에서
진흙탕 속에서
잡스러이 등을 세우며 몰려오고 있어
바퀴벌레와 개미들은 두 손으로 서서
고름 잔뜩 채운 배를 내밀며 뒹굴어 오고 있어
살 위에로 갉아먹듯 스며들고 있어
정오의 사이렌 속을,
배 속을 휘저어 커다란 손으로 끄집어내고 있어
충혈된 두 눈에 가득한 스모그
돌칼 가는 소리, 두 발의 절단된 형벌에의 새로운 꿈
피 흘리는 구세군 종소리에도
놓여질 곳 없는 한 뭉치의 거대한 회오리
회오리 속, 돌풍에 날개깃을 잘리운 나방
가느다란 촉수에서 흐르는 피의 꿈
불구의 눈을 시멘트 바닥에 빼 던져 버리고
잡스러운 무위(無爲)의 통로 위에
끝없는 무형(無形)의 선
피 흘리는 구세군의 종소리만 울리고
끝없는 무형의 선
연달아 끄집어내고 있어도
끝이 없는 무형의 선만이 연달아 흐르는

무위의 통로 위에
바퀴벌레와 개미들은 두 손으로 서서
뒹굴어 오고 있어

산 위에서
구릉지 아래서
진흙탕 속에서

## LOGOS

마음 가장 귀한 곳에
모셔 두는 아름다운 빛

빛이기에,
멈출 수 없는 갈망의 목적

모든 목마름과 메마름의 근원

그것은
위대한 침묵
무언(無言)의 기도

그토록 따사로와
삼키기엔 너무도 고통스러운
눈부심

# 별리(別離)

내속에서또다른나뭇가지에꽃이핀다면
내속에서또다른나뭇가지에꿈이열린다면
별리에더멀리이우주를빠져나가
네가꽃피워놓은나무위에서
네가부풀려놓은따스한해일(海溢)속으로
드러누울수있으련만
내밖을나가지못하는이우주의한복판에서
내밖을꿰뚫지못한채잠을청하는꿈속에서
네게로더욱더깊숙이부드러이닿아가기위하여
별리에더욱더견고히빛나는다리를
영원의기억속에서
네게심어놓기위하여
완성시킬수없는너의詩를띄운다
잠들은네창가에앉아서별리할때엔
새벽이었음을
네기억녘에나는
새벽이슬이될수있겠다
별리와더불은별리의꿈에의
긴항해(航海)속에서

# 봄

행복하시오
얼어붙은 대지(大地)가
활활 타오르는 모태 속에
아리따운 생명의 혼(魂)을 품고 있듯
녹아 흐르는 찬바람 진 것
생명의 기약은 어김없이
어두운 밀실에도 찾아와
헤치고 밀려오는 저들의 발자국
미미한 교향곡 어느덧 경쾌히 울려
가리어진 구석에서
웅크려든 구석,
어두운 상처 입은 것들을 어루만지며
어느새 와,
아이야
문득 고개 들면
모르는 사이
가슴속에 와 불씨를 키우는
곱고 여린 손님네들

햇살이시여!
햇살이시여!
보소서

이 어린 눈빛
게 어딘지 그리워,
추운 동토(凍土)에서
개나리꽃, 진달래꽃 피는 언덕을 기억했음을
보소서
이 어린 눈빛
햇살이 눈부셔
병약한 가슴팍 내밀며
창문을 열어제치움을

# 촛불

촛불처럼 타오르고 싶고,
정신 속으로
영혼 안으로
깊이 파고들고 싶다
그리하여 몰아(沒我)의 경지에서
사물의 본질
생명의 핵심에서
흔들리우고 싶다

詩가 아직 있을 때
살아 숨 쉬는
그 순간, 순간의 의미를
내 영혼의 감성으로
음미(吟味)해 내는 노래를
자연을 창조시키듯
지상의 완전함으로
생성시키고 싶다
내 안에서

거저, 욕심은 없다
내가 원하는 것은
"자유"라는 것으로 인하여

내가 그 안에서 흔들리우는
생명의 본체와
하나가 되고 싶다는 것

소리는 없이 거저,
그것들의 진실을
이해하게 되는
어둠 속의
너를 잃지 않는 것이다

# 학(鶴)


아침에 서걱이는 낙엽 소리에

움츠리는 고독이

살며시 대지(大地)를 밟고

교회의 여명(黎明) 속에 있었다

서글픈 계절이 도시를 잠들이고 가는데

통속하지도 못한 오한(惡寒) 뒤에는

또다시 거기에 서 있는 사랑의 실개울이

새로운 원형(原形) 속으로 내 손을 이끌고 있었다

해변을 서성이다

교과서 어디에도 없는 빵의 부피만큼한

靈의 여로(旅路)에선 항상 짙디짙은 향수(鄕愁)만이

우리의 외로운 백지(白紙)를 채우고 있다


내 책상 위에 있는 너

내 창가의 너

내 손 안에 간직한 사람

내 눈빛을 채우고 간 너

그 쓸쓸하고도 추상(抽象)인 일상에

외로운 학(鶴)으로 날아온 너

바다에 닿아 가기 위하여

패배해 버린 DaDa를

아스팔트 위에서

예지(叡智)로 닦는 너

먼 거리의 종곡(終曲)은 울리우고
외롭게 살아가는 사람들
그 숲에 가리어져
이 어두운 시간을 배회(徘徊)하고 있다

# 새벽


진하고,
깊게,
부드러이 너는 온다

건강한 약속에,
살포시 밀려드는 여명(黎明)의 창가에
너는 청춘의 못다 한 침묵 속으로
뜨겁게 뜨겁게 영겁(永劫)의 빛깔 휘영인다

긴긴밤들의 추위를
따스한 숨결로 뒤엉키우며,
생명의 불꽃을 되불태우며,

노신부의 안경테에 온기 전하며,

마지막 희망의 긴 아픔을
저버릴 수 없는 슬픈 눈가의 사람들에게로,

정의와 진리의 수호신인
하느님의 사랑으로
너는 마지막 희망(希望)으로
그렇게 허기진 우리의 일상(日常)을 빛으로 채우러 온다

# 너

글자와 글자 사이에서도 헤어나오지 못하고
도보와 도보 사이에서도 안주(安住)하지 못한다
그리하여 영상화된 물결 속에서도 떠돌이별이었고
그리하여 나를 이해하지 못하리라
분열되고프지 않으나
거추장스러운 지상의 속도는
메스꺼운 "無"와 행동의 프로그램 사이에서
4차원의 세계로 빠져나가려 한다
나는 내가 빠져나간 공간이다
나는 윤회(輪廻)하는 나무의 수액과 토양이다
내가 빠져나간 공간은 정지(停止) 이외에
침몰되어진 공간 이외에 아무것도 아니다
거기에 리듬과 속도는 없다
나는 지상의 창문에 크게 떠진 눈이다
그 슬프고 황량한 빈혈 걸린 눈이다
한 줄기 글자의 군소집단의 배열은
내 시선 공간의 처음이며 끝이다
나는 소음의 한가운데의 끝없는 고요다
나는 내가 빠져나간 공간이다

# 무상(無常)

절실해도 좋고 절실하지 않아도 좋다
사무치지 않아도 좋고 사무치게 닿아 와도 좋다
어둠 속에서 별을 따라 사는 가난함이어서
생에 소리를 주어도 좋았고
침묵과 정적(靜寂)을 지니어도 좋았다

겨울바다에서 온갖 생명을 잉태(孕胎)하여도 좋았고
긴 우수(憂愁)에 와자지껄한 장터를 읽어 내려가는
어쩐지 견고한 눈빛이었다
잡혀지지 않는 나무의 고독을 지켜보아도
쉽사리 깜박이는 신호등을 따라
재빨리 걸음을 내딛는 시간과 육체였다

그리하여 무엇을 그리워해야 할 것인지
그리하여 무엇을 재창조해야 할 것인지
남기고 가는 의지와 손길들의
뚜렷한 물음들

사무치게 그리워해야 할 것이
이데(Idea)의 허상(虛像)이어도 좋았고
움켜 포옹해야 할 무료한 정경(情景)이어도 좋았다
그 모두가 같은 가지들이어도 같은 분신(分身)이어도 좋았다

많은 것을 내 안에 받아들이고자 해도 좋았고
많은 것을 거부해도 좋았다
그러나,
남는 것은 필연의 굴레, 치밀한 우주의 호흡뿐이다

내가 나를 벗어나고자 해도 좋았고
내가 나를 찾고자 해도 좋았다
내가 나를 못 박아도 좋았고
내가 나와 평행해도 좋았다

그러나,
누추한 껍데기와 본체(本體) 사이에서
물상과 바람은
종소리와 같은 것
사물의 윤곽에서 저음(低音)으로 깔리우는
엄숙한 회복인 것을
구제(救濟)될 수 없는 사물의 윤곽이어도
生은 스스로 흔들리어서 좋았다

내가 너의 외로움이어도 좋았고
내가 너의 고뇌이어도 좋았다
내가 너의 하찮은 계절이어도 좋았다

우리가 물이어도
우리가 스스로 먼 태양이어도 좋았다
아니, 우리가 스스로 먼 돌멩이어도 좋았다

그러나, 生은 여기에 그저 묵묵히
그리고 왠지 두렵게 있는 것
왠지 모르는 원초적인 슬픔이나 삶의 비애(悲哀)처럼
우주의 깊은 정적(靜寂)처럼……

# 폐허(廢墟)

나는 나의 길을 걷고 있었다
내 마음과 혼(魂)은 갈라 부서져 버리는
초겨울의 잎처럼 쇠잔해진
나의 성결(聖潔)을 주워 모을 수 없었다

무덤터에 재생(再生)시킬 수 없었다

나는 울고 있는
창밖의 내 눈빛을 피해야 했다

# 生에게

두 팔을 뻗어 권태와 아쉬움을 뒤로한 채
사라져 가는 당신의 벽(壁)을 잡겠습니다
12월 총총히 설레이는 서울의 야경(夜景)
여물지 않는 가난만이
휘둥그레이 작은 촛불 속에서
우울한 응시로써
슬픈 우정을 띄웁니다
당신의 창가에는 고요하게
때로는 경쾌하게 피리 소리가 맴돌고
순하디 순한 어린 양 떼들이
산마루에서 깊은 밤을 서성댑니다
아마도 그들은 오히려 당신과 친숙하기 때문일 것입니다
설거지통 안에 고드름이 동굴을 이루는
자연의 결정체를 보노라면
아마도 당신의 언저리에는 억새풀이 벌판 가득히
저마다의 율동에서
보이지 않는 무구(無垢)한 혼(魂)들이
자아내는 단조로움만이 있는 듯 합니다
철새들이 한철을 트다 가는 저편 너머
깨끗한 결정체로 깃털 치는 창공은
새로 단장한 명동의 고동색 가로등 위로 머물다 가는
참새들의 차가운 발의 상처를 의아해하지 않는 것처럼

언저리의 잡음은 곧 당신의 전부일 수 있습니다
단조로운 율동은 곧 당신의 전부일 수 있습니다
성가(聖歌) 옆에서 찢어지듯 갈라지는
유행가는 당신의 진실이듯
무수한 혼(魂)들이 자아내는 벤조음은
거칠어진 살갗에 스며드는 평균율의 근원이었듯
흔적도 없이 패어진 반향(反響)
당신의 실체는 자꾸 잡혀지지 않고
근원의 바윗돌 뿌리에서
허허로운 열정은
다함없는 애정으로 가느다랗게 떨립니다

## 정결(淨潔)한 女神

이렇게 두 손을 모으고,
햇살이 스치는 고요 안에
무릎을 꿇고,
내 마음의 영원하신 하느님께
속삭이는 태초(太初)의 숨결을 응시하고 싶습니다

# 어떤 향수(鄕愁)

유년기의 향수처럼
그것은 불현듯 섬광처럼 찾아왔다가 사라져 간다
암흑 속의 자유!
돛을 달고 밤 항해를 떠난 베르나니소스
고독은 아픔보다도 달콤하게 밀려왔고
어느 때의 아이들은 들판에 나가 한나절을 보냈다
딸기 잎새 가시덩쿨 사이로
앙증맞은 꽃뱀이 혀에 불을 켜는 곳
그곳에서 파우스트의 절망하는 지성(知性)의 혼(魂)이 열렸다
한 낮잠 속의 파라다이스는
갈대섬을 건너 별들 곁으로 난무해 갔다
여느 때의 하늘이 끝 간 데 없이 항구를 여는 들판
기류 가득히 새콤한 숨결이 분무한다
거기에 와이셔츠 단춧구멍을 푼
회색의 반항은 존재하지 않았어도
마(魔)의 형형색색의 장식으로 가리운 외로운 生은 없었어도
여느 때의 생명의 씨앗은 햇빛처럼 따사로왔다

# Coffee

별빛 헤치는 창가에서
나무들은 눈에 흰서리가 앉아 있다
밤마다
가로등 불빛은 외로운 양으로 꿈을 잉태한다
거대한 환락의 도시의 복지
복지에 꽃피울 생의 의문들
나는 오늘 Coffee의 향 내음에
나의 도시를 똑바로 바라본다
내게 詩를 놓게끔 나를 키워 온 도시의 마력(魔力)
Coffee 안으로 숨 풀어놓은 내 피곤한 영혼
영혼의 비밀은 그러나 벽 안 쪽으로
밀려나 있어 어두운 암호 문자로 채색되어 있다
詩여! 새파란 눈가의 영원한 청춘의 고뇌여!
고뇌를 담는 네 백발의 순결 속에
떠도는 내 영혼을 잡아다오
무인도에 떠도는 돛배 하나
그 치밀한 생의 허허(虛虛)로움을 위해
나의 잔을 채우노라
가득 채운 이 잔이 넘치고 넘쳐
네 영원한 고뇌의 숨결 안으로
나를 불사르기 위한 것이냐
Coffee 향 내음에

나를 키워 온 도시의 마력(魔力)

떠도는 부초(浮草)처럼

가락만이 맴도는 이방(異邦)이로세

짙고 짙은 안식년(安息年) 짙은 녹색의 끝 모를 고뇌로세

# 나는 고독한 나무의 땅에서 살았네

나는 고독한 나무의 땅에서 살았네
구름 한 점 없는 날에도
응달이 지는 땅에서
개미들이 기어다니지도 못하는
동굴 속에 스며드는
한 줄기 빛만으로
한 쉼의 공기만으로도
꿈과 생명이 피가 되어 끓어오르는
천사의 신음 소리에 이따금씩
쿵, 쿵 뛰는 가슴에
저려 오는 손발을 애무하며 살아왔네

고독한 나무의 땅에서 나는 살았네
기억이 남지 않는 바다 위에서
때때로 먼 항해의 나라로
나는 신의 광기(狂氣)에 고개 숙였고
신의 침묵에 항거(抗拒)했네

그대는
가지 못하는
처형(處刑)의 땅에서
살아 보지 못한 실존의 무게를 거부하고 있을 때

나는 고독한 신의 눈빛을 껴안기 위하여
그분 곁으로 눈웃음 띄우네

개미 밥들, 공든 탑을 뚫는
붉은 흙더미 속에서,
神이여!
고독한 나무의 땅에서
당신 때문에 절망하는
생명의 파르스름한 떨림으로 외로와하지 마옵소서
당신의 기쁨을 위하여,
당신 품 안에서 흔들리는 이유를 위하여,
그 이유의 위대함을 불태우기 위하여,

神이시여!
한갓 생명의 모태(母胎)에서
당신의 오묘하심의 고독을 거두어 가시옵소서

고독한 나무의 땅에서
벌거숭이인 나는 햇빛만을 찾곤 했네
그 찾음의 이유를 위하여

# 예수의 왕국

성대히
모두가 한 형제자매로
갈릴리 호숫가에서 웃음 끊이지 않아
가나안 혼인 잔치에서와 같이
신랑을 맞이하는 새악시의 보드라운 순백한 영혼이었다

그들은 쓰디쓴 쓸개 즙을
예수의 입에 들이대던 날들의
버림받은 저주의 악령들을 짓밟고 선
마리아의 후예들
어린 예언자의 그 험한 가시밭길을 위해
미리 기도로
온 사막을 헤맨
동방의 지혜와 선별들의 영혼
그들의 후예들이었다

온갖 순결한 꽃으로 화관을 엮으리
온 천공의 별들
이날을 환호하며
기나긴 밤에
생명의 뿌리에서 광휘(光輝)에 차며
어린 사람들

촛불 엮어 깨어 춤추리

흩어 내버려진 밀알들

알알이 열매 열려

황혼 녘의 축제를 나누리

길가 버림받은 고아들

가시덩쿨을 뚫고,

햇살에 취해

그때에 한명도 빠짐없이

빛이 스며들지 않는 곳 없어

거지들은 풍요로운 대지(大地) 위에서 춤추고

풀잎 새 이슬로 목 축이리


온 산맥의 정기(精氣)

인간의 마을로 치달아

해묵은 고뇌 위에

더없는 환희의 노래 띄우리


그때에 모두가 하나였음이니

그때에 모두가 하나였음이니

# 몽당연필

꿈을 꿀 권리를 찾아야 하는 지금의 억압과 고통과 더불어
생명을 재창조하는 모든 벌거벗은 나무들은
이미 반을 써 버린 연필로 완성해야 할 데생에
경건한 눈망울의 밤이슬로, 아침의 창문을 엽니다
갈라지는 난음들이 혼자 삼켜 버린 생명의 씨앗처럼
시퍼런 강물의 광란에 충혈되는 두려움에,
스스로의 의자를 만들어 둘 때
풀잎 새에 베이는 도마뱀의 성애(性愛)
신열에 들떠 있는 별꽃들
두 불꽃의 화원에서
바다를 열고
바람의 숨결 속 찰나의 옹달샘을 마시려
어린 사슴의 동공에 푸르른 종소리 깃털 치며
생명의 씨앗으로 은하수 城을 꽃피우려 합니다
은비늘 반짝이는 영혼의 이끼,
원두막에서 홀로 서성대며
정적에 잠길 성화(聖火)에 휩싸여
두고 온 것 있는 양 허전해
반쯤 써 버린 몽당연필로 왕국 없는 왕국을 이루어
그 황홀한 쓸쓸함에 터져 나오는 율동으로
더함 없는 나무들 웃음을 이룹니다

# 箱!

껍데기 없는 그대는 더욱 고독하다
그대의 거미는 그대의 등판
그대의 꽃나무
그대의 아버지의 아버지의 아버지의 아버지의 무덤에서
캐낸 조각난 항아리
그대의 광장은 조각난 항아리였다
조각난 항아리는 그대가 무서워서 달아났던
그 꽃나무,
번식하는 거미

그대는 침몰할 수 없었던 난파선
그대는 희롱당하는 노랑나비
웃음만 있는 탈바가지
클레오파트라의 피라미드를 찾아 떠난 엉터리 건축가

그대의 꿈은 거미였고
그대의 광장은 거미였다

껍데기를 입은 자(者)는 아직 말(言語)이 있다
말이 날아가며 벼랑을 넘는다
말이 그대를 갉아먹는다
그대를 부패시킨다

..............
껍데기도 없이…… 아는가?

# 나비

살(肉) 속에 뜨겁게 꽃피우려
황천길의 개펄을 지나
치욕과 영예의 강물을 건너
온 밤새 울부짖던 못다 한
청춘이여!
설운 순결의 제단에 바친
들국화의 핏빛 숲이여!

모든 인간들에 民主를
그들 조국의 절대 자유를
사모하던 검은 눈동자의 목마름이여!
무덤의 門을 열어젖히고
그대의 열정이 벼랑 끝에 선 살(肉)들에
오랜 날갯짓으로 스물렁거린다

청춘의 모태에 빛나는 월계수여!
그대의 굳게 다문 입술
그 깊은 고독으로
온 밤의 열망을 노래하라
그 성결(聖潔)로
그 환한 피의 요동
길이길이 뜨겁게 꽃피울지어라

# 아웃사이더

生의 어둠을 초탈하기 위하여
禪을 그렸다
무척 저미는 외로움을 더 이상 감지(感知)하지 못하고
나의 어둠은 지상의 포효(咆哮)하는 아가리에 물리었다

얼마나 오래
얼마나 아프게
이 진공관 속에서
바람은 또 그렇게 내 귀로 흘러왔나

무엇이었던가
나의 사유마저도
無처럼 위장한 채
주검을 마시우고
수의를 입고 있었던가

무엇이었던가
실체가 허물을 벗기고
에메랄드 빛
다이아몬드로 빚어져
신의 입김에
투영되었던가……

# 박제(剝製)


한번도충직히내어둠의소리를엮어줌으로난무치못하고
박제된아웃사이더마냥덧없이으스러지는겨울의뼈대처럼
내사모든게허무의덫으로둘러싸여숨소리마저크게쉴힘마저
상실된듯비는이어져쓸데없이추위속으로나락될것이고
날지않는내영혼에지옥인너가예수의손에박히운못처럼
내심장에못을박는다그것도체념과반복에익숙해진
기계적반동에지나지않아모든게끝난것같다

## 영혼의 잠

어제, 난 새로운 젊은 시인의 詩를 읽으면서
짧은 호흡으로 피폐해진 나를 쳐다보았네
그보다도 급히 삶의 패각에 웅크러든 채,
지나쳐 가고 있던 내 영혼의 잠을 흔들어 깨웠네
소생시켰던 봄을 황급히 포대기에 싸서는
어둔 골방에다 내팽개치곤 담뱃불을 지피우는데,
그보다도 진한 내 영혼의 성화(聖火)가
세계와 자아 간 존재양식의 차이라면서
저만치서 홀로 걸어가고 있음을 보았네
그는 사람들 속으로 바람처럼 들어가고,
나는 황급히 도망치고 있음의 차이
단지, 그거였음을 깨달았을 때
오히려 사람들에게 밀착되고 싶은 슬픈 애정을 뒤적거렸네
정경(情景)을 되살려 내는 성자(聖子)의 목소리를 찾아,
그러나, 더 이상 그 곁에서 소생(蘇生)시킬 수 없는
내 영혼의 증류(蒸溜)는
어디에서고 정박할 곳을 쉽사리 찾을 수가 없었네
감옥을 치나쳐 가듯 황급히 정적을 찾아 벌판에 누워 버렸네
보이지 않는 광장은 굳게 닫혀 있었고,
도시의 인부들과 색색의 작부들의, 그 입술의 썰룩거림을
내 눈빛으로 익힐 수 없음으로
나는 남아프리카에 갈 수 없었고,

Show-window 하와이에 갈 수 없었네

아니, 무식한 횡압(橫壓)과 재갈 물린 거리의

이중의 곡예를 벗어나,

사리 몇 조각 움켜쥘 청춘에도,

열려 있는 정신과 사상(思想)의 하늘 밑으로도 갈 수 없었네

다만, 이 우주의 은하수를 첨벙대며 꿈꿀 뿐

내 안에는 원초적인 날개가 있었지만

인위(人爲)의 집은 결코 필요치가 않았기 땜에

# 복도

기억처럼
휘감기는 두 날갯죽지에 파묻은 얼굴
파르르 떨리우는 심장의 복도를
촉촉한 감실인 양 걸어 나왔네
언제고 벽이 있었지만
그 끝에는 사방의 길이 천장을 뚫고
영혼의 바다에로 도망칠 수 있음을 이제는 알아 버렸네
마음은 먼저 달아나 버린
"사랑"이라는 영혼을 휘둘러 보았네
노상, 태양을 쫓는 가난한 손길들과
덮어 놓고 살아 버린 손때 묻은 일상에 숨겨진 웃음처럼
만나야 하는 유성(流星)들의 방백(傍白)을 엿들었지
아, 엉켜진 거미줄의 이슬방울마다 빛과 우주의 프리즘
그런 청명한 시선이 부서져 울릴 때처럼
속삭이는 사랑의 마지막 몸짓을 쫓아가지
아, 어디선가 박수 소리로 꽃다발은 던져져
덩그라니 불빛 속에 짓밟히지
무대 위에 홀로 남은 조명,
주인공은 나오지 않고 객석은 싸늘해져 가고 있었지
무엇이 울리고 있을까?
그대의 몸을 움직이게 하는 미세한 울림들
희부옇게 먼지 날리며 태양은 기울어져 가고

복도 끝에 벼랑이 있지만
사방에로 계단이 있음을 이제는 알지


------- 자막은 알파벳의 왕국을 조립하고 있었다-------
------- End ------- 불이 켜졌다

# 징검다리

30분의 침몰 속에
팔에서 수갈래의 춤이
원시림의 혼(魂)과 나신(裸身)으로 바다에 이른다

그것은 나무 빛깔, 떨어져 나가는 나이테,
솔향기 가득한 낙원의 영생(永生)을 담는다
하나, 둘… 하나, 둘…
못에 박혀 문명(文明)의 꿈을 잉태한다

덴마크는 어때?
거기가 좋을 것이다

헤쳐진 구멍 사이로
또 다른 生이 머문다

바보 같은 창부(娼婦) 같은,
아웃사이더 문학은 어때?

그것은 파열해 버린 둔감(鈍感)의 눈빛
그것보다 더한 정적(靜寂)은 없을 것이다

# 보상(報償)

쉽사리
꿈을 제재(題材) 없는 유형(流刑)의 바다에
잠들게 했습니다
---- 동경(憧憬)하지 않기 위하여----

어렵게 환상(幻想)의 대지(大地)를 뒷걸음질 쳐 왔습니다
-----영혼의 타오르는 황홀을,
　　슬픔을 아는 투명한 육체의 태양에
　　박아 두기 위하여-----

# 사랑

연꽃으로 피어나는 너를 알았다

긴 밤새
홀로 울며, 聖火를 지켜온 부엉이
광년의 바위를 껴안은 물방울의 섬

그러한 그리움의
그러한 목마름의

초록빛 애증을 알았다

# 지나간 시간

나는 지나간 시간 속의 고통과 자유를 그리워한다
아무 상념도 없는 양, 정신은 비극을 느낄 때,
어쩜 가장 행복한 순간을 사는 것이었는지도 모르게
나를 사르어 놓고 가 버린 그 시간의 허무함과
무위인양한 삶의 초루함조차도 그리워한다
정신의 양식을 내 안에 지녔으나 가장 가난했던,
견딜 수 없었던 사막의 모래바람 소리조차도
나는 그리움에 떤다
삶의 아름다움과 고통조차도
나를 나이게 해 주는 비밀인 것을
이제, 나는 그 시간의 비참함조차도 그리워한다
별과 바다와 구름과 그러한 자유의 영역에
나를 바쳐 준 시간을 그리워한다
아니, 보이지 않는 사랑의 힘에
나를 기울인 시간들을 그리워한다

# 청춘(靑春)


다소, 퇴색되지 않는 고유한 자기(自己)를 지니고 있는
그리하여 어떠한 계절에도
항구적(恒久的)인 분위기를 자아내는 것이다
작은 모닥불을 지피우는 영혼의 숨결
오히려 그러한 자유의 해안(海岸), 그 한적한 사랑
詩 안에 깃든 진리의 보상(報償),
순수함을 위한 고통의, 아픔의 대가!
청춘이여!
이곳에 잠시라도 쉬어,
너의 넋을 이 벌판에 눕게 하라
외로운 거북이를 위하여,
우리들 마음의 작은 물고기를 위하여,
촛불의 심지인 양,
허무의 심연(深淵)을 날으고 있는
아이들의 해맑은 얼굴
일상의 무료함을 넘어가는 그 웃음을 기억하기 위하여,
너의 파라다이스에 잠시 눕게 하라
너의 새를 햇살에 뒹굴게 하라
무엇이건
사랑을!
자유를!
꿈꾸는 그 자리에

평화처럼 머물게 하라

# 기형(奇形)

I

아무것도 지니지 않고, 갖고 있지 않다
그것을 행복이라 하는가?

Black-comedy를 갸우뚱하며
Show-window 속으로 빨려들어 가 볼까?
왜?
그냥
재미를 위해서

마천루의 하늘 끝이 보이는 곳으로 올라가 볼까?
음… 따스한 Coffee가 내 빗방울 속 정(情)을 부추길걸…

새로운 왕국의 침실로 가기 위한
열쇠는 지하성당의
낙엽 더미에 파묻혀 있어

그대는
낡은 덧문을 떠밀며,
썰렁한 회갈색의 지평(地坪)에 누워 있었다
오래고…

앙상한 달빛이
펄럭이는 나신(裸身)을 불태우고
오래고…

헌데,
동포의 등굽이 보여지지 않고,
게시판의 기호와 활자가 보여지지 않았다
그것은 죄악인가?
은총인가?

## II

두 촛대를 찾아
다소 울어야 할 것 같은데
황폐해진 내 밀실을 뒤졌지
보이지 않았다

"마치도 그대는
시대의 파편에 얻어맞은…
어용의 혓바닥이었습니다."
"오, NO!"

Bach의 연둣빛 신기루는 춤추지 않고 있는데,
끔찍한 궁뎅이를 흔들지 말아 주십시오
다시금 간통(姦通)을 당하는 시대(時代)의 우수(憂愁)를,
얻어맞은 의식(意識)의 공포 뒤에,
어루만지듯,
神의 빗방울 소리를 들으십시오

이제는 울어야 될 것 같군

그래

울자!

III

불현듯,
순수한 동물로써
인간의 언어를 모르던,
태양 아래 나뒹구는 걸

쪼아 대는 비둘기를 쫓아
벤치에 앉아
현재와 미래의 시간 속에
흐느적이는 내 화살을 당기고 있었다

나는 갈색 피부의 Ja에게
주황색과 연두색의 hi-fashion을 입혀 줄 것입니다
그녀에게 레몬을 갖게 할 것입니다
그녀를 역사(歷史)를 묻지 않아도 되는
열대의 섬으로 데려갈 것입니다
그녀의 눈에 고이는 샘물이
神의 제단(祭壇)에 향(香) 피우는 걸 훔쳐보고 있었거든
그녀의 몸뚱아리가 내뿜는 영혼의 파편들이
바다 한가운데서 맑고 따스한 대기 속으로 뭉게구름꽃으로
이 세상 밖 어디에라도 날아가고 있었지

과거의 반동으로써 화살을 부추기는 거지

만약, (1985년) 하루 10시간 노동에 5000원도 벌 수 없다면
개처럼 일해도 개떡밖에 될 수 없는 거라면
지치고 꿈을 박탈 당한 고립된 병사에게
탄환을 막아 낼 방패가 없다면
피상적인 모든 Ja의 상대적인, 부르주아적인
시간의 무개념적인 양상은
조소와 우롱을 당하더라도
오래고 누워 있을 거다
바람과 태양의 정적(靜寂) 한가운데서

# 잉여(剩餘)인간의 고회(苦懷)

"그녀는 3류치 부르주아의
권태로운, 피폐로움에 빠져들고 있군.
많은 지식과 정서(情緒)로,
잠재울 수 없는 광적(狂的)인 열기로 인하여
생의 원초적(原初的)인 살갗을 지나쳐 갔단 말이지.
항생제에 빠져든 채 언어의 늪에서 졸고 있다니까."

"아, 나로 하여금 끝에 서는 고독을 살게 하여,
영원히 홀로 휘감기는 고둥이게,
심해(深海)의 늪 속으로 빠져들게 하여,
더는 절망일 수 없게
더는 헤쳐 나올 수 없게,
그 안에서 익히우는 과실을 향해
술처럼 타오르게 하여
영원히 불타오르게 하여
그러한 충일(充溢)을 쾌적처럼 살게 하여
Logos를 갉아먹고 사는 나비처럼
커 가는 쾌적을
그 가벼운 듯한 무아(無我) 속으로."

# 11월

밀려왔다, 사라져 가는 해일(海溢)
내 사랑의 념(念)마저도
넌 날 아프게 했다
이제는 아무것도 함께하지 않았다
보채이던 감각의 정경(情景)조차도
아무것도 깃들이지 않았던 심연의 우주(宇宙)
내게 남겨진 것은
허깨비들의 잔상(殘像)에 깃든
짙디짙은 주검의 無일 뿐
빛은 숨을 죽이고
나의 눈빛을 살피우다
홀로 어디론가 이탈(離脫)해 버린 뒤
그처럼 허한 쏘
모든 것이 불연속적이었어도
이전에 나는 너를 믿었었다
상냥한 우주에 깃든 영원한 사랑의 논리
또한, 우주에 깃든 신의 숨결
글쎄
이제, "나"라는 또 하나의 神과
"나"라는 또 하나의 아집(我執)은
어디서부터 헤어지는 연습을 할 것인가
이 밤마저 지새우면

# 쓰고 싶은 이유

I

깨알 같은 글씨로
내 사랑을 주고 싶다
창조주의 것들에게
살아 움직이는 모든 자연(自然)에
이제, 기억에서 지워야 할 죽어 없어진 형체에도
내 사랑을 주고 싶다
나는 부디 오래고 그들을 사랑하고 싶다

生이란
결코 사랑이고,
사랑하는 것 외에 아무것도 아니지 않는가?
내가 그대를
그대가 우리를
우리가 이 세상을
우주가 그의 창조주를
그리고 창조주의 것들을

나는 내 사랑이 우주를 덮고, 바다를 덮고
내 혼(魂)이 사라질 때까지
몇 억겁의 세월 속에

마진(摩震) 속에
불멸(不滅)할 것을 믿는다

## II

나는 사랑하기 위해서 수없이 펼쳐진
활자의 세계로 들어가고 싶다
그 속에서 사랑하는 것들을 위하여
사랑의 집을 지어 주고 싶다
따스한 불길로 그들의 추위를 녹여 주고 위로해 주고 싶다
내 사랑의 입김을 전하며
우주의 외로움과 고통을 몰아내는 것
이 적막하고 비인간적인 느낌들에 부딪혀
진공관 속을 휘젓는 반사적인 나사엽에
자연의 바람 소리를, 빗소리를, 태양을, 이슬을 주기 위하여
"우리"라는 것으로 가난한 이들이 하나가 될 때까지
나는 꿈꾸며
힘 없이 쳐진 너의 어깨 위에
내 작은 손을 건네리라

# 구(球)를 향하여

나 홀로 있는 곳에서
외로움의 씁스레한
그래야 넉넉히 품어 줄 수 있는
너에 대한 사모(思慕)의
막(幕)의 어둠과 빛을 가른 그 속삭임
가벼이
물결 되어 휘영이여
바람결에 묻어나
되살아오는
은총의 삶

어둠이 내리면
하나, 둘,
지피우는
성전의 촛대,
그 응시
그 속에서는
참되이 존재할 수 있으리

무한궤도

# 바다

## I

항상 대하는 바다는 항상 다른 모습으로
가식 없이 품위 있는 자태로
신선한 바람을 몰아
해수면(海水面)에 바다 향(香)을 일으키며
인자함과 질책으로
포근한 사랑의 친애한 품으로써 가까이 밀려왔다
슬플 때 하염없이 기대어 울 수 있는 따스한 바다
그 사랑은 모든 것을 품고 덮어 줄 수 있었다
일치할 수 있는 사랑의 하모니
이제, 눈빛 하나만으로도 전류가 감돌듯 알 수 있는
선량함의 그의 본질
선(善)의 빛이 사라졌다는 것만으로도
삶은 충분히 허망함으로 일그러지고
동지를 잃은 슬픔으로 밀물 치듯이
바다는 지구 위에 정의와 동지애
그 모두를 향한 사랑의 나눔과 소망을 향하여 나아간다
그가 희구(希求)한 인류의 사랑과 빛의 나눔이
우리를 하나로 일치시킬 때까지

II

오랜 시간을 통하여
한 발자욱씩 닳아서 오며
자신의 존재성의 의지를 조금씩 내보이며
농부의 투박한 손같이
가식과 꾸밈없이
항상 광활한 속 내보이며
심금 깊숙이
겸허히 울리우는 바다!

난 오늘도 그의 자유를 찾아가네

# 외로움

많은 밤, 새벽녘, 의식이 깰 때의 순간들

바람과 비와 이슬과
무상(無常)한 지상(地上)의
황량히 젖은 적토 속에서
환생한 듯한 강물 속에서
내 영혼은 항상 그렇게
주체할 수 없을 만큼의
큰 공기의 회오리를
목마름처럼
항상 지니고 살고 있습니다

그렇게,
항상
내 영혼에 접목된
신비한 초목의 울림 속에
그 추상의 감성 속에서
형언할 수 없는
순수한 자연의 본성 속에서
저는 당신 神의 숨결을 들이쉬고
그래서 그것은 사랑이 되고
빛이 되고

어둠과 빚어져
새 생명을 잉태했습니다

# 늪과 비

밀려오는 파도 소리를 내면서 세찬 바람결에
제 몸을 내맡기는 억센 빗줄기들
산다는 것은 몸 붙이고 살기 싫은
낡고 닳아 빠진 이들의 갈라섬처럼
지겨운 습관의 청산과 더불은
새로운 세계로 선택적으로 내몰리는 걸까?

사랑은 단순하고 어눌한,
당당한 채,
무관한 어리석음
실은, 사랑이라는 실체는
주체적 자아의 규명(糾明) 외에 존재치 않으므로
억센 빗줄기의 체념적 극한 상황이 빚어내는
엉뚱한 파도 소리의 연상(聯想)
산다는 것은 살기 싫은 순간의 무한한 인내력의 실험대인가?
존재치 않는 것을 존재케 하는 것의 지겨움이란
어떻게 참아 낼 수 있을까
이 명멸(明滅)치 않을 듯 지루한 시간의 횡포 앞에
무기력함을

# 폭풍의 언덕

블랙홀의 혼불 속에
그를 끌기 시작한다
하나의 춤에 어우러져
그의 영혼에 섞이어진다
불사조의 부활함으로
하나의 피로 이어져 흐른다

# 부재(不在)

사랑의 不在 한가운데서
그 사랑의 눈빛을
기억 한가운데서
붙들고 놓치지 않으려 애쓸지라도
詩가 있어 살 수 있으리라 믿었다

"전구다마의 끊어진 필라멘트처럼 나는 고독하다."고
독백하는 훼밍웨이의
生의 빛을 상실한 고통을 體化하면서

음삽한 냉기로 체온을 잃어 가면서
사랑의 구체적인 임재(臨在)함이 없이
은유를 내포하지 않는
이질적이고
생경한 둔탁한 사물에 에워싸여 있다 할지라도
종교처럼
철학처럼
詩가 있어 살 수 있으리라 믿었다

# 상흔(傷痕)


억지로 말을 토해 내라고 윽박지른들
실어증에 걸린 채,
마음은 빗장을 걷어 올리지 않는다

어둠과 삶, 블루!
생명의 한 과정으로써 받아들여야 하는 긴 소멸, 피 울음…
영혼은 소리 내지 않았다

삭이고 삭인 은빛 광대(光帶)

밀실을 넘어 심연(深淵)조차도 찾아내지 못하는
나로부터 벗어난 핵(核)의 해저(海底)거니,
찬 별들의 소우주(小宇宙)
시원(始原)의 바람

영혼은 사랑이었고
무한한 자기 정경(情景)의
깊푸른 적요(寂寥)만을 품을 뿐이었다

그리고
사랑은 영혼이었다

# 영혼의 시원(始原)


덧없이 사라져 간 꿈 없는 영혼이여!
이슬의 결정이여!
허무의 잎을 키우고
신(神)의 숨결로
밤의 고향으로
찬 별의 생명으로
되돌아가
영원한 안식(安息)으로 환원될지어다

# 그랜드 캐니언

우리가 아직 삶을 다시 시작하기 위하여
자기 앞에 대하(大河)처럼 펼쳐진
광활한 평원(平原)의 생을 향해
두려움 없이 질주할 때
아직 박제된 공룡은 아이처럼
生의 수액으로 새순으로 되살아나
따스한 피로
가난의 희망을
잃어져 가는 행복을
되돌려주었어
긴 겨울 동굴 속에서
예정(豫定)된 신비와 마(魔)의 허물로
절군 상처를 삭여 낼 때에도
불행이 두 눈가에서
웃음을 지워 버리고 있을 때에도
사랑스러움과 천진함의
태양과 비와 바람의 생명은
꺼질 듯한 쇠잔함 속에서도
의식의 파편을 기적처럼 지켜 왔어

# 물아일체(物我一體)


가파르게 깎아내린 절벽의 암석에
뿌리를 드러낸 채 매달려 있는 나무
생존하기 위한 필사의 모습
생명은 존재함을 목적으로 한다는
평범한 원리를 확인케 한다

그 위 벼랑 끝에서 구름 속으로 빨려들어 가듯
하늘과 대기(大氣)를 향하여
너울대는 몇 그루의 나무들

하늘과 구름과 바람과 더불어
그 풍경 속으로 날아 한 점으로 박히고 싶은 나

바다와 나무와 하늘과 구름
대기와 바람
그들 앞에 서면
나는,
나는 더 이상 없어진다

# 백지(白紙)

백지 앞에서 절망감과 싸우기 시작했다
두려움과 무기력함은 패잔병처럼 상흔 속에 싸여 있다
위대한 단순성의 아무 상념 없음은
있는 그대로의 사물이 통과해 갈 수 있도록
흑인 올훼의 거울과 같았다
상처로 얼룩진 랭보의 연민을 떠올리며
펜을 꺾은 그의 청춘의 에스프리를 권하며
나 또한 펜을 꺾어야만 한다는
숨어 버린 詩의 자멸감에
전부를 잃어야만 한다는 역설도 될 수 없는 당위성 앞에
반항할 수밖에 없는 체념을 선택한다
무엇을 위한, 무엇을 향한, 그 무엇도 아닌,
언젠가 스스로에게서 우러나 앙금화될 때까지
그를 기다릴 수 있을까
기다림에 지쳐 퇴화된 속성을 어찌하지 못할 때
과연 버릴 수 없는 연민을 어찌할 것인가
그를 기다리기에는
놓쳐 버려야 하는 그 모든 것의 보상을
아무것도 이룰 수 없는
무위 속에서 찾는 것을 선택할 것인가

# BAN

간 밤에 노곤함에 겨운, 깊은 수면(睡眠)으로
빗소리를 듣지 못했다
아침에도 해돋이를 넘긴 환한 밖의 분위기 깸으로,
여타(餘他)의 아침보다도 늦게 깨어남을 알았다
거실의 커튼을 제치고
홍건히 적셔진 포도(鋪道)를 보고서야
간밤 새 비가 온 걸 알았다
더불어 상기(想起)함으로 뒤척여 대는
여정(旅程)이 없었음을 알았다
실없는 사람인 양 침대 속에서 psychic이 불러내는
불가항력적인 느낌의 긴 줄임표 속,
사랑의 실체에 대한 실험은
갓 구운 빵 냄새 같으면 살이 붙으련만,
진 빠지는 이상심리적 광기의 데미지 같다
상처받기에 익숙해진 영화 속 주인공마냥
급기야는 상처의 와해(瓦解) 반응에 익숙해져 버린 인간처럼,
시공을 초월한 telepathy에 모든 걸 종속시켜 버리기에도
스스럼이 없는 탐미주의자처럼,
움푹 패어진 그의 눈 속에 파멸을 통한 구원과
그리고 그것이 전부일 수 있는 生의 어느 한 시점의 횡포를,
시간의 치유와 망각 기제를 떠올리면서,
이 미친 사랑 극(劇)이 어느 쯤에서

스스로의 극(極)에 달(達)해 꺼져 갈 때,
그 불씨의 잔재마저도
바람과 함께 날려 보내야 할 것임을 떠올린다

## 사랑을 위하여

당신을 사랑한다는 것은
당신의 영혼과 정신과의 합일을
육체의 예속을 통하여 느낄 수밖에 없는
생명의 전부였습니다
밤은 허락지 않는 여건들로 가난한 사랑의 최대의 행복,
합일을 꿈꾸면서 시공(時空)을 넘어서 오는
그대의 영혼과 하나 되어 흐르는
가난한 생명의 전부입니다
당신의 영혼이 나의 육체를 공기처럼 채우며,
영혼을 애무할 때
숭고한 사랑의 절정에 나를 맡깁니다
오늘 밤에도 대양과 산맥을 넘어,
달그림자 진 나의 침실로 스며들어 오는 당신의 자장가 속에
우리의 영혼은 확산되어
이 밤의 신비에 싸인 바다와 창공과 요정의 숲으로 날아갈 것입니다

# 자유

평화의 왕으로 우리 가운데 오신 주여!
우리 한가운데서 당신 자비와 사랑으로써
서로 일체할 수 있는 공동체적 삶을 살게 하옵소서

주여! 사랑의 일체함 없이
스스로의 내면에 불신과 미움이라는
지옥을 살지 말게 하옵시고
당신이 우리에게 가르치는 그 사랑이 누추한 본성을
이겨 내게 하옵소서
주여 당신의 자비로 나를 이끄시고
당신 사랑의 성령과 하나 되어
자유케 하옵소서

내 주 하느님이시여!
내게 영혼 육신을 주시고 나를 기르신 주여!
수없는 불일치와 죄악 한가운데서
나를 불쌍히 여기시어
당신 자비로 씻기소서
당신만이 저에게 참된 진리를 살게 하시고
진정한 자유를 살게 하오시니
주여! 당신의 성령과 하나 되게 하옵소서

# 불꽃의 취기

아직 그대의 언어를 찾지 못했다
사람들 사이에 서면 비껴갈 종이 호랑이 같은 것
그대의 영토를 부여하고
그것이 구제할 수 있는 슬픈 일차원적 삶의 거품을
그 떨구어진 메마른 나날의 풍경에
가벼운 불꽃의 취기를 부른다
무엇으로 인하여 반향(反響) 할 수 있겠는가
가면(假面)의 환태(還態)여
무엇으로 비롯되어
정수리의 우주에 가 닿겠는가
성스러워 슬픈 호흡이여!

# 스침

당신을 "뉘"시라고 부른들
부추기는 연(緣)의 무던함을 이해하지 못하리라
들판의 갈잎이 그러하오리까
애초에
마른 기침 넘치는
인간의 숲에서
진정으로 서러운 눈빛을 보시진 못하시리이다

# Beatrice!

내 마음의 영원한 벗이여!

비가 오는 구중충한 아침에 궁상떠는 두보-
나는 얼마나 그 궁상스런 처연한 두보를 사랑하는가

허무의 처연(凄然)함에
고독의 무거운 추락의 심연(深淵)

거친 비에 휘어지는 나무로 되돌아가
저 비에 쓰러지고픈 아침이다

아무런 말도 고이게 하고 싶지 않은
빈 자아에 텅빈 삶의 정점 안으로
그럴 수만 있다면
오래고 언어는 고이지 않는
직감의 순수 속에 잠겨 있고프다
내 세포 끝에서 느껴 오는 섬세한 감각만으로
철학처럼 존재하고프다
이 아침에 저 거친 빗속으로의 욕망을
실행할 것인가, 말 것인가
비는 날 부르건만
왜 이 도시의 차단된 구역 안에서

영혼만이 설레는가?

나는 얼마나 저 비와 나무와 더불어 행복했던가
들판과 저 거친 비가
나의 오랜 죽마고우인 그들이 날 부른다
이 아침에 미로(迷路) 같은 대륙의 분지점을 벗어나
그들에게로 가기까지
절제된 인고로 세월의 이끼나마
벗어 버릴 수 있을까?

집단 최면과 집단 무의식의
그대의 습성은 저 깊은 숲속에 있다

이 아침에 없앨 수만 있다면 적정한 언어조차도
내 뇌로부터 추방시키고 싶다

열리는 진실의 직관 속에
그러한 원래의 순수성으로 되돌아가
나로 존재하고 싶다


베아트리체!

영원한 로맨티스트!

결국,
자유의 향유의 문제다

종교는 그 절대적 자유로의 입문을
언어를 버리는 것에서부터 시작한다(?)

참된 자유는 참된 자아 해방이다
그것은 나와 세계와 그리고 神이 하나가 되는 과정이고
절대 순수로의 회귀이다

그래서 聖人의 육체와 정신은 그것으로 채워진다
그래서 그곳에는 사랑만이 존재한다

자유로우면 영혼은 사랑으로 채워진다

# 사위춤

그대가 그렇게 살고자 할 때
그대 속에서 그대가 무형의 그대에게
유형의 그대를 소외시킬 때
항상 무엇인가 빠져나가는 듯
진정한 것들의 흔들먹거림을
순간의 정체된 밀집(密集)의 영겁(永劫)을
시간이 빠져 버린 찰나(刹那) 속에서
眞理의 무위(無爲)의 사위춤으로
돌아가 그대임을 내보일 때
그것이 그대의 진정한 현현(顯顯)이다

# 비는 오고

비는 오고
또 그것은 우리를 원래의 삶의 본질을
잠시나마 들여다보게 끔
침묵 속으로
자연에 깃든 감각과 직관 속으로
신의 자유의 공간으로 이끌고 간다

생명은 허무하기에 아름답고,
꽃은 지기에 아름답게 정점을 향하여 만개한다
삶의 이치는 허무함과 참된 자유로움을 함께 지니고 있다
사랑했다는 기억만으로 우리의 연(緣)은 억겁 속에서 빛나고
그리고 그것을 위해 살았다는 것만으로도 삶은 끝없다

너와 내가 함께한 시(時)-공간(空間)은
그 안에 사랑의 기억을 새겨 놓고
다시 되돌아오는 날
그러나 우리의 영혼은 윤회(輪廻)보다도 영원할 것이다

가자 가자!
저 창공으로,
저 대기로,
저 우주로

# 아기 고양이 Kiri!


오늘도 나무 타고 담 넘어
옆집으로 잠입해 갔지
가 봤자 재미없지

Eldery Court!

하루 종일 졸고 있지 않던,
그 할망!

누가 널 애무해 줄까?

엄마 무릎팍에서 자는 게 좋겠지

점심 먹고,

그래

낮잠이나 자자!

# 고독과 외로움을 벗하며

나 자신이 즐기던 고독과 외로움이 생활상으로 내팽개쳐져
퇴행화되어 가는 습성처럼
잊혀질 양 그리워질 때면
짙은 고독과 외로움에 깊숙이 빠져들고파지면,
외로움은 식물성인 이에게 배어 있는,
짙은 초목과 풀잎의 광합성 냄새가 되어
혀끝에서 쓰디쓴 잎 즙과
연녹색빛 차의 씁쓰레함으로 투명하게 느껴진다
헌데, 고독은 노역(勞役)으로 지친 노쇠(老衰)한 육체와
돌보지 않는, 잊혀져 버린, 잃어버린 사랑으로,
더 이상 기다릴 것 없는, 무너져 버린 가슴에,
총명함이 사라진 영혼의 슬픈 눈빛에서
홀로 견뎌진 후미진 절망의 궁방에 퍼진 곰팡냄새처럼
바이러스 침투와 함께 더는 투쟁할 것 없는
구겨진 종이 자락인 양 비비 틀어진 채
뼈마디 마디에 붙은 살조각마냥

고통은 왜?라고 묻는,

술에 절어진 보들레르의 그 크게 패어진 눈두덩이 안에서
극(極)한 정신으로 모든 것을 대변(代辯)하는 듯하다

고독은 언어를 몰아내고 직관과 허무는 그 위를 넘나든다

고독과 외로움을 통해서만 진정으로 정화(淨化)되고
투명한 나로
종교의 의식(儀式)처럼 되돌아올 수 있을 것 같은,
지극히 고양(高揚)된, 인간적인 너무도 인간적인 의식을
되찾을 수 있을 것 같이 여겨지지만,
생존적인 절망의 고독에 빠져 있는
소외(疏外)된 이들의 아픔 앞에서
그것이 얼마나 호사(豪奢)스런 짓거리인지!

# 유영(遊泳)

자유로워지기 위하여
물속에 나를 풀어놓아 본다

태고(太古)의 기억 편에 서면
자유의지의 날갯짓을 익히우던
순간의 불안과 고독을
이미,
자유일 수 없는
절대 자유로의 회귀(回歸)를
창공의 푸르른,
절대 선의 혼연일체(渾然一體)를
이미, 피곤한 지느러미의 처연(凄然)한 흔적에
지나가 버린 향수(鄉愁)를
그려 본다

# Happening

사랑의 시작이 아직 나의 방문턱을 넘어서지 않았건만
난 그와의 끝남을 생각한다
아직 영원을 논하기에는
단순한 흥미로밖에는 받아들이지 않는
별 볼 일 없는 해프닝에
우습게 찡그려진 미간에 하염없는 폭소만 난무한다

한번도 아프면 아프다고 떼쓸 줄 몰랐던 사람이 벗어 놓은
옷섶에서 밤바다의 해일이 인다
神만이 그를 알까?

사랑은 절대합일의 욕구다…
그래서 어쩌라구?

happening은 단지 happening일 뿐인데……

# 여백

내가 살아온 나날은
당신을 사랑하려는 방법론과는 다른 것이옵기에
젊은 날의 비상(飛翔)하려는 관념의 날개로는
당신께 가까이 갈 수 없을 것이옵기에
지난날의 숫기 어린 여백의 투명성은
무서리 치는 대지의 가슴에 영원을 위한
씨앗을 잉태했고
언제고 숭고한 생명의 번식을 위한
사랑의 서곡을 향기로운 꽃들의 제전(祭典)에
뿌렸습니다

# 나이테

아무런 상념 없이 너를 응시한다
내 안에 품기 위하여
너를 알기 위하여

그리고 조심스레이
속삭이기 시작한다

너의 나이테를 보았으므로

# 무한궤도(無限軌道)


길은 막다른 벽(壁) 앞에 막혔어도 좋았다
이미 체념 뒤에 주어진 보상(補償)인 양
초극(超克)할 수 밖에 없는 절연(絶緣)된 것들의
마지막 술잔을 기울면
神은 허허로이
신념(信念) 뒤의 허물어짐처럼
無로 되돌린다

극도(極度)의 피로로움이
뼈와 피의 빅뱅으로
우주의 초신성(超新星)으로 무한궤도(無限軌道)에 오른다
알 수 없는 4차원에 깃든 영속(永續)적인 생명
풀 수 없는 원자(原子)에 깃든 복제(複製)된 기억
그 자력(磁力)의 빛에 빠져드는
아웃사이더!
소생(甦生)의 바다가 그 끝에서
우주 공간으로의 귀의(歸依)를 재촉하며
날 부른다

# 무한 질주(無限疾走)


그저, 끝에 끝을 잡힌 뫼비우스 띠처럼
삶의 윤곽을 벗어나
추적의 막다른 벼랑에서
방사(放飼)의 막으로 되몰려온다 할지라도
끝없는 음모의 유혹을 벗어나기 힘든 불연속(不連續)의 아침
시간의 배수진
神은 가이없고
이제, 마약과 술을 논하고픈 이별
…레퀴엠…
…그라브…
배수진의 시간이 입히울
공모(共謀)된 것의 친숙함
詩의 한 귀절 한 귀절이
영혼을 바다에 던지게 하고
불가지론(不可知論)의 정신이
하나 가득 벽에 춤추어
나를 받아 주는 최후!
나는
비로소
증발(蒸發)하기 시작한다

# 작은 배

항상 그렇듯이
바다의 끝에 서면
긴 역사의 자취로 물들어
투명한 에메랄드 빛 파도와
스카이 블루 빛으로 눈부신 수평선 너머로
한 점으로 사라져 가는 작은 배에
멈출 수 없는 시선을 박고
남태평양의 태양과 하늘과 바람 속으로
홀로 들어가는
영원한 대 침묵의 신비로 적셔진
생명의 사랑을
날아갈 듯한 긴 숨의 습기로 들이키운다
야위듯 얄팍해진 두 날갯죽지의
가벼운 영혼의 돛대로 바람을 타고
물음의 끝에 남는 하느님 전(殿)에
홀로 깨우친 사랑을 찾아가는
작은 배에 나를 띄워 본다

# 묘비명

눈부시도록 아름다운 지구에서 살게 된 것을
기쁘게 생각합니다
빨갛고 노랗게 녹색으로 형형색색 살아 숨 쉬는
자연을 그 품 안에 키우며
파란빛의 테두리로 빛나는 파란 별인 지구
그 생명을 사랑하고, 그 사랑에 넘쳐서 살다 간 사람

어디서나 초목이 있어서 충분히 행복했던,
따사로운 태양의 온정이 있어서 외롭지 않았던,
신선한 대양의 바람만으로도 존재할 수 있었던,
황토 흙 냄새만으로도 일체할 수 있었던,
사람!

자연을 알게 되고 느끼고 그것을 사랑할 수 있어서
행복했던 사람

여기 묻히다

# 절대 자유

자판이초다툼의영감(靈感)을잡을수만있다면좋으련만
순간으로사라져가는바람을잡을수는없습니다
초다툼의神의영역에깃든당신을느낀다는것은
찰나(刹那)의해탈(解脫)이었습니다
대자연의절대순수속에깃든
당신의존재에가닿는바람결이었습니다

# 나부끼는 풀잎

사랑과쓸데없는성정(性情)의줄다리기를하다
한갓되이나부끼는풀잎이된채
사랑의큰은하계의만유인력의중력속에흐름을타노라면
같이있지못해죽을것만같은사랑조차도
손아귀로부터빠져나가기시작하는바람이래도
그모두가나의것이아니어도스스로흘러가는生은
또다시무덤덤한나로되돌아온다

제3부

원소(元素)

# 원소(元素)

......

......

......


그렇다 하더라도 내 젊은 날,
이미, 묵시적 공유함으로
찌는 알제리의 작열하는 태양과 더불어
일찍이 인생의 허무함을 통두리째 껴안고,
태양과 바람이라는 원소들과 더불어
그들 안에서
더 이상 아무것도 묻지 않으며
그들처럼 원소로 화(化)하여
진정한 자유로움으로 남으리라던,
그 허무 속에 깃든
참된 자유로움으로 존재하리라던
실존을 뒤적인다


우리를 무기력하게 울게도 한 저 부조리(不條理)한 세계와
잠시 거(居)한 까실까실한 모래로 씹혀지는 세계로부터
우리의 진정한 고향으로
우리가 잠에서 깨어 수긍(首肯)한 사랑에로
그 동지애로

정신의 고향으로 귀의(歸依)하리라 다짐했던
거짓 없는 실존(實存)을 끄집어낸다

# 육체(肉體)

일생을 "사랑"이라는 단 하나의 원소로 인화(印畵)하고
자신의 고독을 눈꽃으로 채운 채
실낙원을 꿈꾸는
상처 입은 영혼의
홀로 영원히 절대의 자유로움에
자신의 춤으로
언제고 자신의 안식과 고유의 빛 안에서만
숨 쉬려하는
그러나 지치고
그리운 정신의 본향이여!
자신 이외의 불순한 것들을 받아들일 수 없는
무소의 뿔로 굳어진 정신에
감미로운 새들의 정겨운 지저귐도
이슬에 젖은 풀잎과 야생화의 선율도
그리움과 충만함으로 나의 육체 안에서
그들의 페이지로만 남으려 할 뿐
사랑이라는 일상의 빵이 필요한 울타리 너머의 키다리에게도
울화병을 가슴에 생채기로 저미고 사는
그저, 치매에 걸린 죠니와 별다를 게 없는
타성의 반동으로밖에 존재치 않는
상처로 곪은 이들에게도
육체를 바쳐 사랑한 神을 등진 채

언제나의 사랑의 기제를 빼어 버린 듯
보이지 않는 너에 대한
또 다른 神에 대한
사랑의 법을 되묻는 작은 소우주(小宇宙)
쓰는 글만큼 그가 "나"라는
보이지 않는 날개를 지닌 者라는 걸
사랑이라는 단 하나의 정직한 육체를 통해 비쳐 본다


--- 神이 나에게 육체를 바쳐 인간을 사랑하기 위해 오신,
　　神의 사랑을 받아들여, 자신을 버리고,
　　죽이는 법을 터득하게 하셨다면,
　　나는 해방되어 진정한 나를 찾았을까? ---

# 나는 바다로 가는 길을 알고 있다

은밀한 비밀처럼
내 마음의 전부인 바다
生의 끝 지점에서
내가 최후에 다다라야 할 바다
그곳에 다다르면,
生은 비로소 내 영혼과 정신의 합체(合體)로 충일하고
온전한 신의 사랑으로 충일(充溢)한 곳
生의 끝 지점에서 영원(永遠)으로 이어지는 곳
생명의 반열에 이르는 곳

나와 똑같은 영혼으로 존재하는 너
똑같은 자유의 의식으로 하나가 되는 너
존재의 주어짐으로
영원한 無의 영원한 있음으로
이제 함께 영원히 있을 너

나는 바다로 가는 길을 알고 있다

오랜 상처와 비극 한가운데서 익혀 온 너

오랜 이 꿈이 다 지워지면,
이제, 되돌아가야 할

나의 본향(本鄕)인 너

그래서
나는 바다로 가는 길을 알고 있다

----진화하는 영적 생명의 감각,
　　그 기적 같은 빛의 환희에 싸여
　　섭리와 신비에 깃든,
　　이 허무한 우주의 심장
　　영혼의 바다에로----

# 눈물단지

하느님을 생각하면서
항상 나는 울고 있었다
生의 외경(畏敬) 속에
生의 광장(廣場)을 생각하면서
또 그렇게
노상 울고 있었다

# 내 주, 하느님!

나로 하여금,
당신의 아름다움에 취하게 하시고,
흠숭과 찬미의 산 제사(祭祀)에
분향(焚香)케 하옵소서

# 혼자서

의식에는
근접할 수 없는 비애(悲哀) 같은 것이 있다
상처처럼
공유되길 거부하는
굳이 치유받길 거부하는
그것은 혼자 가길 원한다

교묘한 문명의 이기 속에
문화적 논리로 채색된 슬픈 자화상들

굳이 위선과 속됨의 비루함에
타협하지 말고

사랑의 자리에로
근접할 수 없는 비애(悲哀)인 양

혼자서 가자

# Bea!

아무리 취해도 취해도 모자라는 것이 있다
그것은 아름다움의 현혹(眩惑)이다
그것은 나의 영혼을 먹이고
적시운다
그것을 굳이
당신의 모든 것을 바쳐
인간으로 오신 하느님의 사랑이라 부르리라

하느님은 최상의 아름다움이시다

그분은 나를 자유케 하시며,
승화(昇華)의 탐닉 속에
生을 무위(無爲)케 하시리라

내 주 하느님이시여!

당신을 위하여
당신이 내신 이 삶의 순간순간 속에서
당신을 위하여
되돌릴 수 있는
생명을 허락하시옵소서

# 히스크리프

"나를 두고 죽은 그녀를 용서할 수 없다."
"나는 기도 하겠다. 신에게
그녀로 하여금 안식치 못하고 떠돌게 해 달라고
내가 죽을 때까지."
"그녀의 영혼이 유령(幽靈)이 되어서 내 주위를 맴돌게 해 달라고…."
"그녀가 없는 세계에서 나는 살 수 없다."

캐시의 죽음을 전해 듣고
나무에 머리를 박으며,
절망감에 짐승처럼 울부짖는 히스크리프
히스크리프의 맹목적인 사랑이
캐시를 유령(幽靈)이 되어 폭풍의 언덕에 머물게 한다

사랑은 아무나 하는 것이 아니다
사랑은 영혼이기 때문이다
미치지 않고서는 아무도 사랑할 수 없다

# 향(香)

내 아름다운 님을 위한 향연(饗宴)은 퇴색되고
그처럼 그리움은 바람결에 마지막 향(香)의 잔재를 날리우고
하늘에서 별이 떨어지는 날에
여류시인의 물고기들은 더욱더 짙푸르러지고
내가 사랑한 당신은 그러한 것들이
당신의 눈 안에서 보석으로 찬란하려니와
당신을 사랑한 이유는
당신 눈 안의 빛 때문이고
당신을 사랑한 이유는
당신 안에서 그 모든 것은 보석이 되기 때문이거니와

이제
당신을 놓고
잠시 가려니와
님은 항상
나의 시원(始原)이거니와,
끝이려니와
그래도 잠시나마
안녕히……

# Nature

이처럼이나
마음이 상실한 채,
동결(凍結)된 감각으로는
너를 느낄수 없다

마음의 온기를 복구하려 한다

사랑의 잔재만으로
DNA를 복구한다

수없이 가느다란
염기배열은
긁혀진 채
수액 밑으로
삶은 넋을
잃어버린 채
시공간(時空間)을 가둔다

나는 너를 느끼고 싶다
너에게 내 사랑을
표현하려 하지만
얼굴 근육조차

움직일 수 없다

마음은 고향을 찾아
항상 피곤했고
그리고,
항상 떠나 있었다

# 유령(幽靈)

생각해 볼래?

삶은 정확한 논리를 원한다
아니, 나는 정확한 논리적 사유를 원한다

왜, 유령처럼 떠도는가?
유령처럼
가야 할 곳도 모르는 채

그러나,
안다는 듯이 엷은 미소 짓지만
아직,
논리가 정립되지 않았다
실은, 뇌 한쪽이 게을러서
사유를 거부한다
속 시원히 이렇다 할 단순 명료한 설명을

너는 원하는가
삶은 싱겁다
너에게는 혹독하고 쓰다구?

나날은 많고

내일 아님, 그 너머에서 생각해 보지……

내가 왜?
유령처럼 이생을 떠도는가

왜? 그처럼 의식과 영혼에는 방이 많은건지
망각한 듯 살지만

그럼에도 항상 사랑이 있어
그처럼 뜨거운지

# 이주(移住)

길들여지는 것과 익숙해지는 것
가장 두려운 것은 상실감
익숙한 것들을 뒤로 한 채
길들인 것들을 잃어버려야 하는
미아(迷兒)처럼 새로운 세상으로
어쩔 수 없이 밀려나야 하는
두려움과 낯설움, 불편함
정신이 닻을 내릴 수 없어
이주사(移住史)는 유쾌치만은 않다
실타래 풀 듯 미로의 섬으로 들어가듯
무엇을 잃고, 버리고,
무엇을 추구하여, 가는
뼈대는 애시당초 묻어 버리고 아무런 근원도 없고
약간의 우울함은 커피에 탄 프림같이
태양 아래 멈춰지고
녹여 난 숙명의 휘어짐
지구촌…
그러나 대양(大洋)만 한 거리감에서
상실감의 진정한 실체도
알고프지 않은
상실감으로
그 낙원에서

마음을 안아 주고
영혼을 돌려줄 시간을 그리워하고 있었다
그렇게,
몇 해의 계절을 나와 내 아이는
아무도,
No touch하는 그 땅에서
멸종위기의 자연과 생명을 소중히 지키고
키우는 그 낙원에서
애틋한 새끼 고양이 kiri가 심리적 안정과
애착을 지녀 갈 때
우리의 마음과 영혼도
자유로운 공기 속에 소소한 일상의 느긋함으로
그 무결점의 순수한 자연으로부터
남태평양의 바다와 태양으로 그슬려지고 탄탄해진 채
대양의 바람으로 채워지고 있었다
……
그곳은 그곳만의 접혀진 채 끊어진 페이지로 있다
다시금, 이어 써 가야 할,


순수한 자연 속에 깃든,
미약(微弱)한 생명들과 만나는
그 행복감,

그 설레임으로,

하루해를 넘기는……

# 죠르바

바다에 나가
투명한 태양 아래
바람과 대기와 함께 춤을 춘다

드디어 희랍인 죠르바가 된 듯
비로소 소외되지 않은 삶의 뼈와 살이 된 듯

神만이 지닌다는
절대 자유의 공간으로
희열의 빛으로
꿈꾼다

# 먼동

온 밤새
온몸으로,
온 맘으로
너를 기다린다

주술과 마법의 악몽으로
이식해 놓은 암흑의 혼돈
잔혹하고 비정한
천박한 종(種)들의 전쟁에
결코
더 나아지지 않는
이성(理性)과
인공 지능에도
먹통 된 채,

통로는 단 하나

이 모든 걸 정지시킨 채
너에게로 가는 길에
먼동이 트누나

# 마음의 양식(糧食)

# 生의 한가운데서

삶은 말을 없애고 뭐랄까?
사막 한가운데서 맞이하는 칠흑 같은 밤의 냉기와
무성(茂盛)한 먼 본향(本鄕)의 분신(分身)인
별 무리만을 벗 삼아도
충분히 외롭지 않은, 순례의 무곡(舞曲) 위에서
고장 난 기구와 단절된 통신으로
되돌아갈 수 없는 어제의 일상이래도,
한낮의 고열을 동반할, 삶의 희망이었던 태양의 광폭함으로
아침을 맞이해야 하는 두려움과 타들어가는 갈증과
모래 날리는 소리 외엔
환청만을 들어야 하는 극한 상황의 연속이래도,
그 극한 상황의 지속되는 반동을
견뎌내 왔던 생의 여지(餘地)로
정신만으로 비애같이 묵중한 삶을 대신한다

삶이란 그런 것이다

--- Vivaldi, 가장 좋아하는 그의 명증(明證)한 음악들은
　자유로운 영성(靈性)의 천재성으로 빛난다
　영감 inspiration, 온전한 집중 그의 선율은 그런 것이
　다 ---

삶은 그런 것이다 칼릴 지브란의 시귀대로

"삶은 고독한 바다에 떠 있는 작은 섬이다.
그러나 그대의 섬에도, 나의 섬에도,
아무도 다다를 수 없다."
..............
"그대의 어둠이 아무리 깊어도,
이웃의 등불은 그 어둠을 밝혀 줄 수 없다."

궁극적으로 삶은 혼자서 견뎌 내야 하는 것이다,

노동 해야 한다
생존하기 위해선
당분간 노동 시장에서 허우적대는 시늉이래도 해야 한다

산다는 것은
책임질 거리를 스스로 만들고 선택해서
그 책임에 코 꿰듯이
타성에 절은 수레바퀴처럼 그렇게
굴러가는 것을 막을 순 없다

노동해야 하고 당분간 또 나를 잊어버린 듯 살아야 한다

나로 되돌아오기 위해선
노동절이 끝나고 안식절에 들어서야 한다
그 안식절이 올 때까지 의식도 정지 상태에 들어간다


항상,
바람은 불고
눕기 좋아하는 나는 주위의 여건만 주어진다면 어디에서고
항상 안식년의 긴 일광 의자를 찾는다
차라리 풀밭과 태양 광선만으로도
너무나 좋은 더 이상의 장소는 없을 것이다


자신 스스로를 벗 삼아서 사는 것
산다는 것은 그런 것이다
아름다운 나의 아기가 있고
그것도 아름다운 자연이 있고,
음악이 있고,
훔쳐볼 수 있는 아름다운 그런 인간적인 지성(知性)이 있고,
뭐 그래서 홀로서도 잘살아져 가는 것이다


알프스 소녀 하이디처럼
동화처럼 단순하고 순수하게 살고픈 희망사항이다

그러나,

사랑에 대한 미련을 버릴 수 없다

막연한 사랑에 대한 기대와 꿈 같은 것,

그것은 그 사람의 체온일 것이다

사랑은 그 사람의 체온과 체취만이 줄 수 있는

안식 같은 것이다

나는 그래서 사랑에 대한 꿈을 재수정한다

이제는 그 사랑의 체온과 체취를 찾아내고 싶다

누군가를 사랑하고 획득하고 싶다

사랑을 찾고 그리고 그 사랑을 찾아낼 때

비로소 사랑하기 시작하는 것,

마음을 다해

아직도 늦지 않으리

미지(未知)의 그 사랑을 찾아낸다는 것이……


행복해지기 위해선

완벽한? 사랑을 찾아내는 것이다

나의 완벽한? 동행자를 찾아내는 것이다


노동하고, 사랑 찾고, 애 보고,

그렇게 우리의 생의 시간은 흘러간다

토마스 머톤이 정의하기를
영혼은 지성과 사랑이라고 했다

우리는 우리의 영혼을 보기를 원한다

아름다운 영혼
영지주의자들

피와 살을 섞어
영혼까지 가져갈 사랑을 하지 않는다면 그것은 무가치하다

그러나,
과연 절대 순수한 사랑을 할 수 있기나 할까?

오로지 사랑만이 남아서 영혼으로 무한히 날아오를 뿐이다

# 화살기도

화살기도의 위력을 체험할 수 있을까
기도의 신성한 능력을 믿어 의심치 않습니까
기적을 바란다는 것은 아닙니다

기도의 힘에 나를 맡기고
그분에게 모든 것을 내맡기우고
가자!
그래
무소의 뿔처럼 혼자서 가자

더욱 빈번히 더욱 많이 화살기도를 하자
하느님을 사랑할 수 있는 더욱 많은 시간을 갖게 될 것이다

기도할 때마다, 난 그분의 아름다움에 빠진다
하느님은 기도를 통하여 우리의 영혼을 정화시키시고
하느님의 신비에 빠지게 한다
하느님은 멀리 있는 게 아니고
바로 내 안에 내 영혼의 길을 통하여 계신다

하느님을 체험하고 그분의 아름다움을 느끼기 위해서라도
기도하는 순간순간을 지녀야 하겠다

# 공동선(共同善)

더는 기다릴 수 없는 순간에도
오랫동안 사랑의 예의(禮儀)로써
너를 기다렸다
마음 한구석은
아마도 예의(禮儀)를 생각하면서
기다림에 지칠 때쯤
너를 망각하기 시작했다
사랑이 예의를 지니려 할 때
이미 나는 너를 벗어나기 시작해서
집착으로부터 자유로워지기 시작했다

너와의 일체감으로 내 생이 채워지기를 바라던
순간은 너무 길었고
맹목적으로 너를 보고 싶어 하는 시간은
마치도 生은 그러기 위해서 존재하는 듯했다

이제 나는 너를 지웠지만
그러나 너에게 감사한다
너는 내 몫까지
열심히 살아야 하겠지
너와 나의 삶에서 서로가 무관해지는 대가가
너의 행복 때문일 테니까

그리고
하느님의 자비와 은총이 항상 너와 함께하길 바란다

"사랑이란 너의 행복에 기초한다."
사랑의 간격이 항상, 우리 사이에 냉정한 정신으로서
너의 절대적 신앙처럼 있었다
사랑은 항상 냉정했다

반드시 많은 이들의 눈물을 닦아 주는
영성(靈性)의 위대한 빛이 되길 바란다

아마도 같이 있으면 안 되는 이유가 그것 때문이었을 테니까
그것을 "공동선"이라고 부르고 싶다
나는 공동선이 개인의 행복보다 우선해야 한다고
항상 생각했다
·················

# 참을 수 없는 존재의 가벼움

참을 수 없는 존재의 가벼움으로
어딘가에 숨겨져 있는 그 사람의 따스한 바다에 이르면
오랜 허구와, 지치고 피곤한 기만의 정서에
드디어 휴식할 수 있는 고향의 온전함에로 귀의한 듯하다
우리를 지켜 주는 대의명분(大義名分) 같은 것
詩, 정치, 영화, 열린 사회,
희망하는 미래 사회를 염원하며,
우리 모두의 사회적 대의명분 같은 것이
우리를 살아가게 하는 유일한 끈인가?
참된 외계는
절망하는 내계적 인간의 허무를 지탱해 주는가?
무엇이 우리를 살아가게 하는가?

참을 수 없는 존재의 가벼움,
사회적 유대감이
나를 부추기는가
사회가 나를 살게 하는가?
언제고 그것으로부터
도망갈 채비를 하고 있으면서도
왜, 사회는 또한, 사회적 대의명분으로 우리를 구속하는가

인간적인 얼굴을 한 경제!
인간적인 얼굴을 한,
가장 냉소적인 물욕처럼 버티고 서 있는……

우리가 해결해야 할 과제가
무슨 명분의 합리성으로 나를 기만하는가?

꿈이란 나누어야 할 그 무엇인가
혼자 하는 세상이라면 벌써 거덜 났을 세상을
가장 비사교적인 인간에게
가장 유대감을 지니게끔 아직도 관심사의 영역에서
나를 구속하고 있는가

# 상대적 사랑

상대적 사랑은 편하다
합리적인 사랑은 절대적인 상처를 받을 일이 없으니까
사랑은 그대를 소유하는 것만은 아니다
자유롭게 해 준다면서 행동반경을 넓혀 주는 것만으로는
자유를 주었다고 할 수 없다
자유를 무슨 정조의 일탈이라고
봐준다는 것도 웃기는 일이다
연인을 진정으로 사랑하려면
그의 자유를 인정하는 것에서부터 시작해야 한다면서
대단한 무소유의 경지에 이른
진정한 사랑을 하는 연인이라고
착각하는 기만은 자신 없으면 관두면 되지 웬, 역겨움

사랑은 무소유를 실행하는 척하는 것인가
소유 못해 피 말리는 싸움인가
사랑은 에로스도 사랑인가
사랑은 정신적 플라토닉만
사랑의 이름으로 존중되어야 하는가
남녀 간의 사랑은 이기적 성욕의 생리학적 수식어인가

중요한 것은 사랑은 마음의 확산이다
정신 작용으로 반쪽과 반쪽들이 합쳐져서

온전한 형태를 이루려는 것이다
사랑하는 연인에 대한 끝없는 동경과 같은 것이다
사랑하는 연인의 영혼과 합체되는 것이다
소유욕에 불타서 숯 덩어리처럼 까맣게 되는 것이 아니라
합일하지 않으면 견딜 수 없는
존재의 참을 수 없는 가벼움인 것이다
이룰 수 없는 동경처럼 사랑의 꿈을 꿀 동안
당신의 영혼이 연인의 영혼을 애무하는 것이다
연인의 육체 안으로 들어온 사랑의 에네르기이다
그 사랑의 힘으로 연인의 전부와 형태를 지니는 것이다

# 거품

너무도 많이 지껄여 대는 게 거품이다
그 쌓이고 넘치는 말들의 홍수 속에
항상 침묵하려는 것은
내 말을 더 보태고 싶지 않아서다
심정적 접근에서부터
주위와 그리고 본질적인 삶에 관련된
만상과 사물을 인지하고 싶다
항상 너무 많은 말들에 치여서,
심정으로 그들을 느끼고 인식하려 하는 것
그것이 자신이 항상 사물과 사람들을 대하는
원초적이면서도 가장 본질적인 것이다
심정으로 접근하고 사물을 감지하고 인지하려 하는 것
마음의 울림과 영혼의 느낌으로 인식하려 하는 것
그것이 자신이 세상의 사물을 대하는 법이다

말을 놓는 그 순간부터 마음은
내적 정신의 온유함으로
더한 사랑의 빛과 대기를 지닌다
그래서 침묵은 선의 빛으로
온전해지는 길로 가는 길목 같다

하느님은 왜 침묵하게 하시는지

왜 항상 비워 버리게 하시는지
그것이 하느님의 사랑법이다
침묵은 그분의 사랑법이다

온전해지기 위해서
깊은 산속 홀로 휘어지는 안개마냥
나 또한 홀로 휘어지고 싶다
나무는 그저 거기에 있고
흔들리는 것은 너와 나의 구별이 없다

무슨 선(禪)문답이냐
니가 웬 선승(禪僧)?
당장 들어가서 침잠(沈潛)하시지
우주의 심연(深淵) 맨 밑바닥으로
첨벙!

## 마음의 양식(糧食)

오늘 또 찾아내지 못했다
내 마음의 양식(糧食)
오랫동안 허기졌다
그러나 어디에서고 마음의 위로를 찾아내지 못했다

여름 휘파람새는 어디 있을까?
정신의 위대한 스승들은 다 어디로 숨은 것일까?
빵처럼 당신들이 필요하다
『명상의 씨앗』토마스 머톤이 필요하다

내가 사랑한 위대한 스승들은 이제 내 곁에 주어지지 않는다
혼자 견뎌야 한다
生을 사랑하는 방법

Young!
너의 허상도 아무런 것도 해 줄 수 없다
하느님의 은총이란 게 이런 게 아닐까

자신의 본질을 아는 것
하느님의 은총을 깨닫는 것

이냐시오 로욜라!

우연히 이 위대한 영성을 접했다

영혼이 메마를 때
관상적 차원의 신앙으로 넘어가길 원할 때
사랑으로 꽉 찬 시선의 온유함으로
사물을 응시하고픈
그러나 다시 처음으로 되돌아가 묵상(默想)으로
내 이성(理性)의 빛으로
하느님의 진리(眞理)와 아름다움을 사색한 후에
수없는 기도의 습관으로 나를 관성화한 후에
관상으로 들어가야 함을 알았다

# Secret!

삶의 고통으로부터 벗어나고자 하는 이들에게
종교는 마약과도 같은 것일까?

각종 질병들
각종 아픔들

고통은 왜?

괴로울 때면 주! 예수 그리스도를 바라보라

십자가형에 매달려 극심한 고통으로 신음하며,
손과 발에 대못 박히우신 예수
창에 찔려 물이 흘러나오는 그의 옆구리
가시관에 눌려 피로 뒤범벅된 그의 머리
비아냥과 놀림과 경멸의 소리가 그를 에워싸고,

그토록 무능하신 神의 아들

그분의 전부이신 神으로부터도 버림을 당하신 듯한 예수

모든 것으로부터
버림을 당하신 듯 철저히 홀로이신 예수

예수의 왕국은 어디에?

이교도와 같았던 우리가
이스라엘의 하느님을
받아들이고 그를 섬김은
그가 전지전능하시고 천지창조 이전부터 존재하셨던
하느님이시기 때문이며,
그가 사랑의 제국에 우리를 불러들이신 까닭이니
저가 홀로 칭송받고자 함이다

"우리를 긍휼히 여기사
곤궁함과 핍박으로부터 구하시고,
부조리한 세계에서 자유롭게 하시옵소서."

"원수가 항상 옭아매려
송사 짓거리를 도모하며
저들의 우상에게 무릎 꿇게 할 짓거리를 도모하오니,
주여!
당신의 방패와 창, 검으로 그들을 꺾으시고,
그들의 비아냥과 웃음거리로부터 구하시고,
환난 날에
하늘과 바다가 온 천지에로 둘러싸

방패 되게 하시옵소서."

자신이 하는 일이 하느님에게로 되돌아가는 일이 아니라면
하느님의 뜻에 부합하지 않는다면,
하느님으로부터 복을 받지 못할 것이다

기적을 바라는가
이적을 행하길 바라는가

믿거든 구하고
기적을 체험하여라

그는 거저 주실 것이다
차고 넘치도록 주실 것이다

구약에 보면,

---인생의 성공은 하느님의 강복에 달렸다는데,

어떻게 하면 하느님의 장자의 강복을 받아
자손에게까지 창성한 복으로 충만할 것인가
어떻게 하면 하느님의 복을 받아낼 것인가?

성경에 이르길,

"내 시작은 미약하였으나, 내 나중은 창대하리라."
"누구든지 나를 믿는 자는,
나를 보내신 이를 믿고, 그분을 받아들이는 것입니다."

"먼저 너는 그의 나라와 그의 의를 구하라."

"아무도 어린아이처럼 되지 않으면 하늘나라에 들어갈 수 없다."

"아버지 이 사람들이 모두 하나가 되게 해 주십시오."

"나는 여러분의 곁을 떠나갑니다.
그러나 여러분에게 성령을 주고 갑니다.
불안해하거나 두려워하지 마십시오."

"이 세상 끝날 때 까지 나는 여러분과 함께 할 것입니다"

"나는 여러분에게 평화를 주고 갑니다.
내가 주는 평화는 세상이 주는 평화와는 다릅니다
불안해하거나 두려워하지 마시오."

그러므로, 우리 안에 그분이 거하시면
하늘나라는 우리 안에 있는 것이다

삼위일체이신 주 예수를 구세주 그리스도로 영접하고,
믿으면 강복을 받게 되는 것이다

# 창조(創造)


모든 물속화(物俗化)되고,

거짓과 가식(假飾)의 우상(偶像)으로부터

자유이고자 했던 사람,

고고(孤高)한 삶의 순수기류를 타고,

고독한 자기로부터

투명한 지상의 새벽을 지켜보던 사람,

진정으로 자신을 살고자 했던 사람……

젊은 날의 삶의 지표처럼,

존경과 일체감으로 따르고 싶었던 사람, 시몬느 보봐르!

그녀의 투철한 자아의식과

타협하지 않는 신념적인 삶의 자세는

무엇보다도 관념과 절대 정신으로 혼란해하며

천상과 속진 사이를 오가며,

방황하며, 돌파구를 찾던 나에게

희미한 광선처럼,

본질의 숙명처럼

중용(中庸)의 도를 구현(具顯)하며

삶을 재현하는 그녀를 통하여

그녀가 사는 모습을 삶의 기준으로 삼고자 했던,

그리하여 이 아름답고 찬란한 태양이 내리쬐는

삶을 긍정하게 해 주었던,

위대한 승리자였던 그녀는

진정으로 성실하고 거짓 없는 위대한 철학자이며,
구태의연한 인습과 편견에 찬 사회의 가치관과
도덕으로부터 벗어나 한 인간으로서
여성의 진정한 실존적 가치를 몸소 실현하려 했다
그녀에게 있어 실존의 최대 가치는
진정한 자기로 사는 것이었다
때문에 양육되고 주입된, 전통적이고 고전적인 개념의
여성의 미덕을 답습해야 하는 수동적인 여성으로서가 아닌,
자기의 삶에 적극 개입하고,
주관적 가치와 역량으로
당시대적 삶에 적극 참여, 투기하는 것이었다
그것은 그녀에게 있어 창조적인 저작활동으로 표현되는데
기존의 관념적 세계관으로부터 벗어나
실존의 조건과 상황을 비판적으로 수용함으로써
자신이 속한 사회와 세계에 적극 개입, 참여함으로써,
어떻게 살고 투쟁해야 하는지
그녀의 저술을 통해 여실히 보여 준다 하겠다
그녀가 고전적이고 전통적인 여성으로서가 아닌,
불합리하고 탈 의식적인 인습으로부터
자신을 발견하고, 주체적인 삶을 일궈 내기 위하여
냉철한 지성과 투철한 의식으로
자신의 이성(理性)에 의하여 검증되지 않은

기존의 사상과 가치를 거부하며,

그 누구를 위해서가 아닌, 자신을 찾고 지켜 나가기 위한,

자신이 주인이 되는 삶을 살고자 했던 것은

철학적 고뇌였을 것이다

그것은 실존주의의 진실이며,

이성의 힘으로써

자유를 향한 삶을 살려고 했던 것으로 내게는 각인되었다

그러한 그녀에게 가장 큰 힘이 되어 주고

버팀목이 되어 줄 수 있었던 것은

그녀의 위대한 사상적 정신적 동반자였던

Jean-Paul Sartre의 격려와 지지(支持)였을 것이다

# 수행(修行)


그대가 그대의 몸으로 완벽하게 존재하는 것을 실행하는 것
매 순간을 완전히 깨어 있게 하는 것
지금, 하는 행위 하나하나에
하찮아 보이는,
특별한 의식을 필요로 하지 않는 것일지라도
그대의 전부를 집중하는 것
그것이 수행이라 했다


항상, 그럴 수만 있다면
그렇게 호흡이 머무는 그곳에서 존재하도록
나를 붙잡아 두고 싶다


그러나 나는 항상 나를 떠나서
떠돈다

# 안식일(安息日)

어떠한 변명도 허락되지 않습니다
아마도 제가 가장 사랑하는 것은 하느님입니다
하느님을 가장 사랑한다면서
교회에 가지 않는다는 죄책감에서 해방될 수 있을까요?
시몬느 베이유,
그녀가 교회에 가지 않은 이유는 무엇이었을까요
영세하지 않은 대부분의 인간들 때문이었을까요
그보다는 자신의 철학적 진실과
객관성의 고찰 때문이었을 것입니다
예를 들면, 창조 신화를 받아들일 수 없는
그와 유사한 창조 신화의 원형들이
타 종교에도 있었기 때문입니다
하지만 그 누구보다도 가장 선량하게 살다간
그녀의 가난한 영혼을 존경합니다
그녀의 가난한 영혼, 인식에 바쳐진다는 것은
아마도 매 순간을 그렇게 살다 간
그녀를 두고 하는 말 같습니다
매 순간을 철학적 고찰과 인식에 바치고
자신의 양심대로
진리대로 살고자 했던

우리의 삶에는 매 순간을

자신의 깨달음의 생각을 현실화하는 것이 어렵습니다
옳다고 여기는 것을 위하여
자신의 여력(餘力)을 바칠 의지(意志)를 실행하기가
너무 힘듭니다
그녀의 영혼은
암울했던 시대(時代)에
한국 여성들에게도 요구 시 되었던 인물입니다
누가 시대의 양심을 책임질까요
누가 휴머니즘을 위해 자신을 바칠까요
우리에게는
그러한 지성(知性)과 영혼이 절실히 필요했던
시절이 있었습니다
아니, 영원히 필요합니다
이제, 우리는 긴 터널을 뚫고 나왔습니다
하지만 아직도 우리는 시대를 지켜 줄
등대(燈臺)의 불빛을 원합니다
우리는 아직도 가야 할 길이
우리 앞에 끝없이 펼쳐져 있습니다

하느님을 만나지 않았다면,
"나"라는 인간은 아마도 사랑이 없는 길고 지루한 곳에서
아무런 희망의 빛도 발견할 수 없었을 것입니다

그것은 헬렌 켈러와도 같은 세계였을 것입니다
어둠 속에 아우성치는,
순결한 빛에 싸인 자연의 프리즘 기적(奇蹟)을 모르는,
이성(理性)이 깃들지 않은,
절망적 상황이었을 것입니다

하느님은 사랑입니다
그 사랑은 구원(救援)입니다
많은 이들이 이 오아시스를 만나길 바랍니다
하느님을 만나지 않았다면
그처럼 아름다움의 근원이신 하느님을
깨달을 수 없었다면
내 삶은 아무 희망이 없었을 것입니다
하느님은 희망입니다

그렇지만,
하느님이 공기라지만
하느님이 호흡이라지만
그렇지만
저에게 안식일에 혼자 있는 것을
허락하여 주십시오

그대를 사랑할 수 있는 것조차
거짓일 것입니다
왜냐하면 사랑은 내 시간의 할애(割愛)이며 움직임입니다
구체적으로 나를 쏟아야만 합니다
사랑은 나를 주어야 하는 것입니다
그렇지만 나는 그대에게 나를 할애(割愛)하지 않았습니다
사랑을 말할 수 없습니다

또한 사랑은 모든 두려움을 몰아내는 것입니다
사랑은 세상 끝날 때까지 함께 하신다던
하느님의 약속입니다
하느님의 사랑처럼
우리의 사랑도 사랑하는 이의 곁에 머무르는 것입니다
마음을 다해
온 정성을 다해
사랑에 자신을 쏟아 주어야 합니다

자신을 무(無)로 돌린다는 것입니다

# 사랑의 시작

사랑은 타인의 상처를 보다듬고
사랑하는 것에서부터 시작해야 한다

아무도 정신적 외상으로부터 자유로울 수 있는 인간은 없다
때론 기억에서 없애 버리고픈 상처는
기억도 찾을 수 없는
해저(海底) 속에 묻어 두어야 한다
영원히 끄집어내지 마라 영원히
정신과 샘이 뭐라 씨부리까도
그 상처는 앞으로의 더 많은 삶의 시간과 경험과 지혜가
언젠가
스스로 자유로울 수 있을 때
스스로 치유될 것이다
그것이 스스로 자유로와질 때까지
망각하자
어차피, 생은 이어져 가야 하고

"상처 받지 않은 영혼이 어디 있으랴." -랭보-

때론 산다는 것이 지옥이다
이 지옥을 견뎌야 하는 형벌이다

# Love, Seeking that Light

## Table of Contents

Part 3

# Elements

✦

Part 4

# Nourishment of the Heart

✦

# Part 1

# Impermanence

# Sound

You,
Deep within your sorrowful heart and body,
Amidst the antinomic sound of life,
You wake up in the morning, and in the evening,
You lie down in front of the wall
   where the sound is dancing

Amidst countless entanglements
In the lonely and weary sound,
Another sound emerges,
Tears trickle,
Laughter resounds,
Taking shelter within the romantic melodies
Roaming and dancing franticly, the sound of life

You nurture the blade of grass  inside your body,
Fluttering in the wind,
Washed in the river,
Follow and live along the sound deeply rooted
   within you,
Seeking the freedom nestled deep
In the melancholy, solitude, and gaze of the flesh

The harmony all those sounds,

Everything hidden within that harmony

And the sound within me

# Mountain

Always, approchinging like a mountain
   and becoming a mountain again and again
Fields, the sound of fields weeping from afar
The sea, run barefoot into the sea

Sound! A sound in your flesh
You become a mountain and echo resounds

You shouldn't seek anything anymore

One who go deep into alone!

Become a mountain

Sometimes, go to the sea
And live there like that!

# The Forest

Covered behind fallen leaves,

Our vapors

Together swallow in anguish,

Dew-drenched leaves,

Countless young mountain birds coo affectionately,

Soothing their longing,

Far away,

Steps of shabby affection in the near invisible days

Sunlight a bit more,

Upon a small hay pile,

Sunlight a bit more, within secretive shades,

Above the deep nest,

To meet, deep within the mountain,

Alone, bending like swirling mist,

Above our steps of shabby affection······

## Us

For a long time, we hid our bodies in sadness

In the shadows,

Under the stillness of the sunlight,

Our tears,

Went to the sea, and make a same one dream

I saw that our sadness made our silver-shimmering
  dreams dance


We saw our sadness dancing as a glistening dream


Our souls were passing by in the waves,

Our souls rising into even greater waves,

Within a single blue wave


Night,

Now, in this darken night,

Witness their raging dance,

From here to there,

Approaching each other,

See the forms of their yearning to meet

# Mirror

In that mirror stands the Saint-Narcissus,
  the spiritual me in the silence of a sickened time,
There lies the loneliness of someone
    I can't stop missing
Finally, in the wandering that needs healing,
  a desolate touch of love was hidden
Narcissus! his forehead so pale and green,
  familiarity matured within his solitude,
The light of truth was too bright,
  and the soul encased in melancoly so felt too light
In his naive yet comical gestures,
  a matured forehead narrates the rebirth of peace
Now, it seems even in his winter, spring will come
His temple, his altar,
    bedecked with purple and yellow flowers,
    heralding his season,
Together with him, I have lived through
    so many seasons


But now, tears must cease to exist
In this spring, let's bid farewell with smiles
Smiling, let us realize the brilliance of new love

Now, I long to embark on an adventure and gamble
  towards the reality that offers only one path
Shedding my somber clothes,
    I crave to breathe the fresh air
Thus, in that mirror, let pinkish white clouds, clear
  skies, and boundless seas bloom abundantly

Sea! Let's set sail like a transparent soul
    longing for the sea,
With an innocent, immature laughter embracing us
    like soft feathers
So homeless, diving into herself,
For the gypsy girl, let's play song wordless ballads
Further more, let's raise our glasses in a warm toast
Like an ignorant child, holding a bouquet
  in both hands, with a flutter of skirts,
Let's walk on the river's edge
Let's love that modest soul

Ah, in spring, like snowflakes swirling
    in profound stillness,
Let's bravely recognize that winter's pain was white

Let's boldly leap towards a life where the beginning
and the end reside on the same straight line
Thus, gazing at myself in the mirror,
our souls united in love
Becoming the breath of warm spring
Let's bestow laughter upon the boundless sea and
the deep blue sky······

# Night Street

Come to here
Lying within the wind
  carrying the fragrance of flowers,
In this street
  where the isolated shadows of people vanish
As the night deepens,
Even our unhideable hunger grows deeper
The colder the handful of starlight becomes,
The murmuring gaze, alone,
Above the spreading dark night sky blue,
In the embrace of the dancing blue butterflies'
  fantastical shadows

Like that, come to here,
With hair untangled,
Shimmering like silver scales,
Within the body of a swallow,
Spewing countless streams of water

Our isolated shadows,
When the green breaths grow faint,
Trying to sink deep into the gaze that floats,

In the wind we longed to roll in for so long,

Drinking the dew

# Solitude

All paths are open
    to the vast sky of the sea and fields
Oh, heart!
Do not yearn in vain for the understanding
    and proper recognition of others
What you should rise above
Even in their hands,
Away from the noisy ears and flattery,
Go far, into the vast expanse

A Zen mind fondly embraces sheep
    grazing peacefully in the meadow
Those distorted, unsatisfied harmonies of life,
From the aimless streets you walked,
And the disfigured faces of the city,
Surely, they were just your young steps
A futile prayer of a lonely heart,
Believing that even amidst those sordid
    and trivial noises,
It could find something

The scent of a lonely late spring,

Amidst the dried-up echoes,

Continues its faint steps toward the dawn,

Regarding the melancholy abandonment of all things


Oh, heart~

Hum your gentle song,

Open to the vast sky of the sea and fields,

Through all the paths

# Abyss

## I

Beauty lies
In the empty heart,
In the sighing of grass leaves
Within the shadowy wind

The mind resists vigorously
When boredom disappears
In the repetition of rhythm
To the beautiful body that falls asleep

In the space not completely submerged,
A language blooms abundantly,
In the forest of language,

The light of the bare body

Flames flicker without elasticity,
Shadows of unfamiliar thoughts do not appear,
An unfamiliar house
Tears of the unfamiliar deep sea

Tears of language

Without dance,
In a place with no house of language

Fiercely unfamiliar,
Eyes filled with wonder

Even the grass leaves,
And the loneliness brushed by the wind,
They do not exist there

They do not exist there

## II

As if hiding,

Unrelated to anyone,

Even gods not invited there,

Though eternal flow may not exist in eternity,

Through an existing name,

Any language can live,

Yet no language can be the true essence


We untie a new language,

Celebrate the space of a new language


At the end of suffering,

Nailing the pole of eternity,

The agony of the islands reaching into

The new life,

Remembers only one essence


Freedom!

Freedom!

Freedom,

Firm,
Solemn,
With love…

## To Live

To live means :

To gaze at the lives of others,

To suffer until only bone dust remains,

To fall into  the unfilled empty abyss,

To get a soul from the confines of nothingness,

To retain the whisper of soul
   perched on a swaying tree,

To walk on the maze searching for a definite name

## Eucharist

He

always,

At that time,

In the cathedral,

Sitting in the last row,

Would gaze endlessly at the Eucharist's flame

Yearning for soaring,

In unity with the eucharist,

He dreams⋯⋯

# Traces

Everything will become mere bubbles

All the past amusements, decorations, and pretenses

On the streets, on the streets

On the rocky ridges connecting mountains and cities,

Ultimately, life buried in that city,

Organized,

Creating contradictions upon contradictions

That violate the essence of being human


When I hold onto my existence,

I can see your existence shining through,

My light can behold you

With your face against my chest,

When your weeping pain stirs my heart,

We all become a handful of clear morning dew


While the fierce waves crash upon the rocks,

And the calmness returns,

We are once again caught in the storm,


We become one light

We become one light

# Cartwheel

On the mountain,
Under the hillock,
In the mud puddle,
Hastily erecting their backs, they gather
The cockroaches and ants,
   standing on their two hands,
Extend their oozing bellies,
   rolling towards us
Seeping into our flesh as if gnawing,
In the noontime siren,
Digging up stomach and pulling it out
   with massive hands
The smog filling blood-shot eyes,
The sound of sharpened stone knives,
   new dream of severed limbs,
A colossal whirlwind with no place
   for the bleeding Salvation Army bells,
Within the whirlwind, a moth with its wings
   torn off by the storm
The dream of blood flowing
   through slender tentacles,
Casting off disability eyes onto the cement floor,

Above the wretched path of non-action,

Endless formless lines,

Only the ringing of blood-dripping

   Salvation Army bells,

Endless formless lines,

Continuously pulling out,

Endless formless lines flowing

   one after another,

On the path of non-action,

Cockroaches and ants,

    standing on their two hands,

Rolling towards us


On the mountain,

Under the hillock,

In the mud puddle

# LOGOS

A beautiful light
Held in the dearest place in the heart

Being light,
An unstoppable longing's purpose

The origin of all thirst and drought

It is
The profound silence,
A wordless prayer

So warm,
Too painful to swallow,
Blinding brilliance

## Separation

If flowers bloom on another branch inside of me,

If dreams open up on another branch inside of me,

I will venture further into separation's universe,

From the tree where you bloomed flowers,

To the warm sea where you swelled,

I could lie down there,

But in the midst of this universe,

   unable to leave its boundaries,

In a dream where I cannot penetrate

   beyond my exterior,

I strive to reach you more deeply,

With a bridge that shines more brightly

   in separation's brilliance,

In the eternity of memories,

To plant in you

An unfinished poem that I float

When sitting by your window,

   seeing your asleep,

   at that time of separation,

It must have been dawn

In your memory notes,

I could become the dew of dawn

Together with separation,
   in separation's dream,
During the long voyage

# Spring

Be happy
As the frozen earth
Carries the tender soul of vibrant life
Within its blazing womb,
The melting chilly breeze flows
The promise of life inevitably
Finds its way even in the dark secret chambers,
The footsteps of those who are rushing through
A minor symphony resonates as briskly as ever
In hidden corners,
In huddled corners,
Gently caressing the wounded and darkened things,
Suddenly, it comes,
Oh, child!
Suddenly lifting your head,
Without realizing it,
In the heart, a spark ignites,
The precious and delicate visitors

Oh, sunlight!
Oh, sunlight!
Look here

This young gaze
Longs for somewhere,
Remembering the hill
   where forsythias and azaleas bloom
In the cold frozen land

Look here,
This young gaze
The sunlight is dazzling,
Sticking out weak chest,
Opening the window

# Candlelight

I want to burn like a candle,

Deep inside my mind,

Deep within my soul

And in that state of selflessness,

I want to sway

in the essence of things,

At the core of life


When there's still a poem

Living and breathing,

In that monent, I want taste

The meaning of each passing moment

With the sensibility of my soul,

Creating a song as if crafting nature,

Forming it into the completeness of the world

Within myself


Without greed,

What I want is to become one

With the essence of life,

As I sway within the realm of "freedom"

In silence,

Understanding the truth of those things,

In the dark

I will not lose you

# Crane

In the morning,
Amidst the rustling sound of fallen leaves,
The crouching loneliness
Gently illuminated the earth,
Within the dawn of the church
As the melancholy season puts the city to sleep,
Behind the unrelenting chill,
Once again, there standing the stream of love
   leading me into a new form
Wandering along the beach,
Not found anywhere in the textbook,
In the journey of the soul,
   as vast as the volume of bread,
Only deep nostalgia fills our lonely blank canvas
On this abstract and lonesome journey

You on my desk,
You by my window,
The one I hold in my hand,
The one who fills my gaze,
You, the lonely crane, flying into
This desolate and abstract everyday,

To reach the sea,

Polishing the defeated DaDa

With wisdom on the asphalt

The distant finale resounds,

The lonely people living on,

Hidden in that forest,

Wandering through this gloomy time

# Dawn

Boldly,
Deeply,
Softly, you come

With a promising vigor,
Gently gliding through the window of dawn,
You enter the unspoken silence of youth,
Radiantly gleaming with the colors of eternity

Embracing the coldness of the long, long nights,
Entwining with warm breath,
Reviving the flames of life,

Gifting warmth to the old priest's glasses,

To those with the lingering pain of last hope,
To the sad-eyed people who can't let go,

You come as a tender light of love,

A guardian of justice and truth,
As the love of God,

As the final hope,
To fill our hungry daily lives with brightness

# You

Unable to escape between letters,
Restless between footsteps,
Thus, I was a wandering star
   amidst the visualized  waves,
Hence, you may not understand me

Not desiring to be fragmented,
Yet, The cumbersome speed on the ground
Seeks to escape into the fourth dimension,
Between the nauseating "nothing" and
   the program of actions

I am the space I have left behind,
I am the sap and soil of the reincarnation tree
The space I have left behind is nothing
But a space submerged only cessation
There, there is no rhythm, no speed

I am the wide-open eyes on the window of the earth
The sad and desolate eyes afflicted with anemia

An array of the letters small units

Marks both the beginning and end of my gaze

I am the boundless tranquility in the midst of noise

I am the space I have left behind

# Impermanence

It's okay to be desperate,

and it's okay not to be desperate

It's okay not to be yearning,

and it's okay to eagerly hope to be one

Living poverty, following stars in the darkness,

It was okay to give a sound to life,

and it was okay to keep silence and stillness


It was okay to conceive all kinds of life

in the winter sea,

Reading the crowded noisy traditional market

in long melancholy,

There was somehow steadfast gaze

Even observing the ungraspable loneliness of an tree,

It was the time and the body that quickly stepped

along the blinking traffic light


And so, what should I long for?

And what should I recreate?

Distinct questions left behind by will and touches


It was okay to ardently longing for even the illusion

of the metaphysical Idea,

Even the monotonous landscape that I have to adore

Even if they were all the same branches,

the same alter ego

Even if I wanted to accept many things within myself,

And even if I wanted to reject many things

However, what remains is the wheel of necessity,

the meticulous breath of the universe


It was okay for me to escape from myself,

And it was okay for me to seek myself

It was okay for me to nailed myself

And it was okay for me to paralleled myself


However,

Between the humble shell and the essence,

All things and the wind are

like the temple bell sound,

Laid with a bass tone in the outline of things,

like a solemn recovery

Even if it's an outline of things

that is beyond redemption

Life was good because it shook itself

Even if I am your loneliness,
Even if I am your anguish,
Even if I am your trivial season,

Even if we are water,
Even if we are distant suns by ourselves,
No, even if we are distant pebbles by ourselves,

However, life is here, quietly embedded
And somehow being afraid
Like an unknown primal sorrow
    or the pathos of existence,
Like the profound silence of the universe······

# Ruin

I was walking my path
My heart and soul shattered like frozen leaves
     in early winter,
I couldn't gather the pieces of my sanctity

I couldn't resurrect them in the graveyard

I had to avoid my tearful gaze outside the window

# To Life

Leaving my boredom and regret behind,

I will stretch my arms and catch your vanishing wall

The night view of Seoul, fluttering in December,

Amidst the immature poverty,

I send sad friendship with gloomy gazes,

In small charming candle light

Peacefully by your window,

Sometimes cheerfully, the sound of flutes echoes,

Gentle young lambs roam the mountain ridge

   through the deep night

Perhaps they feel familiar with you instead

If you look at the crystals of nature,

   where icicles form caves in the dishwasher

Likewise, in your surroundings,

   the meadow is filled with reeds,

There's only the monotony created by

   the invisible innocent souls in each movement

Beyond over, the sky flutters with clean crystals,

The migratory birds flying away higher

On the newly renovated Myeong-dong's streetlights,

No one wonder how cold wounded feet of sparrows

The clamor of your surroundings may be

your entirety,

The monotonous rhythm may be your entirety

Just like the popular songs torn apart beside

    the hymns are your truth,

The Banjo sound played by countless souls,

Once permeating rough flesh as the root of

    the average rate

Splashing echoes without a trace,

Your essence is not captured,

From the root of the fundamental rock stone

Empty passion quivers slenderly

    with endless affection

## Pure Goddess

With my hands clasped together like this,
In the tranquil embrace of the sunlight,
I kneel down,
Longing to gaze upon the breath of the beginning,
Whispering to the everlasting god of my heart

# The Nostalgia

Like the nostalgia of childhood,
It comes and goes like a fleeting flash
Freedom within the darkness!
Bernanos setting sail, guided by the stars,
    on a night voyage
Solitude came sweetly, even more than pain,
And the children of that time spent a day
    in the fields
Amidst strawberry leaves and thorns of wild vines,
A charming little snake ignited a fire with its tongue,
There, the despairing soul of Faust's intelligent mind
    was revealed
In a brief slumber, paradise crossed over
    to the stars,
A usual sky opening the harbor
    onto the endless plain
Filled with currents, a tangy breath mists the air,
Even if there were no rebellious gray
    with his shirt unbuttoned
Even if there were no loneliness was hidden
    behind fancy decorations by superstition

As always, the seeds of life came ripening

like sunshine

# Coffee

By the window, where starlight splashing,
The trees are adorned with frost in the eyes,
Every night,
Streetlights conceive dreams in lonely sheep
The welfare of a huge vulgar-colored city
Life's questions blossoming in welfare,
Today, in the aroma of coffee,
I gaze directly at my city
The black magic of the city that raised me
   to discard poetry
My tired soul released into the coffee,
However, the secrets of the soul are confined
   within the walls,
Colored in dark cryptic characters

Oh, poetry! Eternal agony of azure eyes' youth!
Seize my wandering soul,
Drifting in the pureness of your silver hair,
   which contains agony
Like a sailboat adrift on a deserted island,
Fill my cup
For the emptiness of that meticulous life

So this cup, filled to the brim, overflows,
To set me ablaze within your eternal agony's breath?

In the aroma of coffee,
The magic of the city that raised me,
Like floating weeds,
I'm a stranger with only a tune
A dense and profound sabbatical year,
Into the boundless agony of deep green

# I Lived in the Land of Lonely Trees

I lived in the land of lonely trees

Even on a cloudless day,

In the shade

The ants can't even crawl

Seeping into a cave

With just one ray of light

With just one breath of air

Dream and life boil into blood

An angel's groan makes my chest thumped

   occasionally

I've been caressing my numb hands and feet


I lived in the land of lonely trees

On the sea that I can't remember

Sometimes to distant lands of voyages

I bowed my head to the madness of God

I resisted the silence of God


You are

Unable to go

In the land of execution

When you're rejecting the weight of existence

that you've never lived
To embrace the eyes of the solitary god
I'm smiling with eyes beside him


The Antsbob,
    that breaks through the hard-working tower
In the red dirt,
God!
In the Land of the lonely trees
In despair because of you
Don't be lonely with the blue tremors of life
For your pleasure,
For reasons that sway in your arms,
To burn the greatness of the reason,


God!
From the matrix of life
Take away the solitude of your mystery


In the Land of the lonely trees
Being naked, I used to only look for sunlight
For the reason of its search

# The Kingdom of Jesus

Majestically,

As one big family,

Laughing endlessly by the shores of Galilee,

Rejoicing like at the Cana wedding feast,

A pure, innocent soul, like a first little lamb

They trample upon the cursed spirits

Of those bitter days when they forced the bitter bile

   into the mouth of Jesus, the forsaken curses

They were descendants of blessed Mary

For the a thorny path of the young prophet,

They prayed in advance,

Wandering the desert in search of

Eastern wisdom and souls of good stars

They were the descendants

They will weave garlands with all pure flowers,

All the stars in the sky

Will celebrate this day with joy,

In the long night,

Filled with radiance from the roots of life,

Young people will awaken and dance,

Scattering scattered grains,

Each seed will bear fruit,

Sharing in the twilight festivities

Orphaned children by the roadside,

Breaking through the thorny vines,

Intoxicated by the sunlight,

At that time, not a single one will be left behind,

No place untouched by light,

Beggars will dance on the bountiful land,

Their throats moistened by dew on grass leaves

The vital energy of the entire mountain range,

Flows into human settlements,

Upon the old aged sorrows,

Songs of unparalleled joy will resound

At that time, everyone will be one

At that time, everyone will be one

# Almost Used Pencil

Amidst the oppression and suffering of the present,

Where all bare trees must seek the right to dream,

To recreate life with half-usedpencils

To complish the dessin

All bare trees

Open the window of the morning

With the night dew of the reverent eyes,


Like seeds of life swallowed by cracking noises

In the madness of the sepia river, swollen with fear,

While crafting own chairs

Lizards mating on blades of grass,

Star flowers excited by fervor,

In the garden of two flames,

Open the sea,

To drink from the fleeting well of the wind's breath

Into the young deer's pupils,

   chirping with turquoise bell feathers,

The seeds of life bloom the Milky Way Castle


Moss of souls glimmering with silvery scales,

Wandering alone in the thatched hut,

Enveloped in the stillness of the holy fire,

Feeling empty, having left something behind,

With half-used pencils,

creating a kingdom without a kingdom,

Through the rhythm bursting

with enchanting loneliness,

The boundless desperating trees restore laughter

# Sang!

You, without a shell, are even lonelier

Your spider is your back

Your flower tree,

From the tomb of your father's father's father's father,

You unearthed a fragmented jar,

Your square was a fragmented jar

The fragmented jar was the flower tree

    you were afraid of and ran away from,

Breeding spider

You were an unsinkable shipwreck,

You were a mocked yellow butterfly,

A mask with only laughter,

A fake architect who left to find Cleopatra's pyramid

Your dream was a spider,

Your square was a spider

Those who wear shells still have words,

Words fly and cross the cliff,

Words bite you,

Corrupt you,

………

Without even a shell…… Do you know?

# Butterfly

To bloom a hot flower within the flesh,

Passing through the celestial path of abalone shells,

Crossing the river of humiliation and glory,

Crying all night

Oh, the unfulfilled youth!

Offered on the altar of pure innocence,

You, the crimson-blooded prayer

    of wild chrysanthemums!

Longing for democracy in all human beings,

Their country's absolute liberty

Oh, the thirst of black-eyed pupils!

Pushing open the gates of the tomb,

Your passion flutters around the edges of the cliff,

With long, long wings, it wanders

Oh, moonlit laurel shining in the womb of youth!

Your firmly closed lips,

With that deep solitude,

Sing the yearning of the whole night,

With your purity,

The surging waves of your bright blood,

Endlessly,

Bloom fervently

# Outsider

To transcend the darkness of life,
I painted Zen
No longer sensing the deeply piercing loneliness,
My darkness was bitten by the roaring gills
   of the world

How long has it been?
How painful it has been?
Within this vacuum tube,
Did the wind once again flow into my ears?

What was it?
Even my thoughts
Disguised like nothingness,
Drinking the death,
Wearing the shroud of hemp cloth

What was it?
The essence shedding its husk,
Emerald light,
Formed into the diamonds,
Projected by the breath of the divine

# Taxidermy

Unable to dance with my sound of darkness,
   faithfully
Like a taxidermied outsider,
Like the winter's crumbling skeleton, all of me
Enveloped by the snare of emptiness,
   even my breath seems loud
Struggling to breathe, it feels like strength is lost
Rain continues to fall, connecting into a meaningless
   stream, into the cold,
In my unflying soul, you, hellish being, drive nails
   like a nail in Jesus's hand into my heart
Even that becomes nothing more than a mechanical
   reflex, accustomed to resignation and repetition
It feels like everything has come to an end

# Soul's Slumber

Yesterday, I gazed at my weary self with short breath
  as I read the poem of a new young poet
Yet, more urgently, I shook awake the slumber of my
  soul that had been crouching in the shell of life,
  passing by
Hastily Bundling up the resurrected spring into
  a hasty packet, I lit a cigarette in the dim room
Yet, more than that, as if the profound beacon of
  my soul was a difference
Between the world and the form of existence,
I saw it walking alone far beyond
He enters into the people like the wind,
While I, in the difference of urgently escaping
Only when I realized that, I fumbled for a sad
  affection that wanted to cling to people
Searching for the voice of the Saint who brings back
  the scenery
But, The distillation of my soul, which can no longer
  be resurrected by the side,
Couldn't easily find a place to anchor anywhere
Hastily seeking stillness as if breaking through
  a prison, I lay down on the field

The invisible square was tightly closed,

The twitching lips of the city's hard workers

and the vulgar bar's

I couldn't familiarize myself with them

through my gaze

I couldn't go to South Africa,

I couldn't go to the show-windows of Hawaii

No, I couldn't escape the double acrobatics

of ignorant oppression and muzzled Streets

Even grasping a few Sarii-beads, Buddha's relics,

of the youth,

I couldn't go under the sky of open spirit and ideas

I just dream of splashing the Milky Way

of this universe

There were innate wings within me,

But the house of artificiality was never needed

# Corridor

Like memories,

Buried in the outstretched wings, a face

Walking through the corridor of a shivering heart,

As if in a moist hideout

There were walls, long ago,

But now I've come to know that beyond them,

    through the ceiling,

A path in all directions can lead to the sea of the soul

My heart looked around the soul named "love"

    that had fled first

Always, the poor hands chasing the sun,

Like the laughter hidden in the daily life

    covered with handprints,

I listened to the side stories of meteors

    that must be encountered,

Ah, dewdrops on tangled spiderwebs,

    each a prism of light and universe

As if that clear gaze shatters and resonates,

I pursue the last gesture of whispering love

Ah, somewhere, applause sends bouquets flying,

Illuminating the darkness

Alone on the stage,

The protagonist doesn't appear,

    and the audience grows cold

What is ringing?

The subtle vibrations that move your body,

Dust flies a pale blue, and the sun tilts

At the end of the corridor, there's a cliff,

But now I know there are stairs in all directions


------- Subtitles were assembling the kingdom of

    alphabets -------

------- End ------- The light turned on

## Stepping Stones

In the sinking of 30 minutes,
The dance of the water striders from my arms
Reaches the sea with the spirits of the primeval
    forest and naked flesh

It carries the color of wood, the falling annual ring
Filled with the fragrance of pine,
    it contains the eternal life of paradise
One, two, one, two···
Nailed to the stake, it conceives the dream of civilization

How about Denmark?
It should be nice there

Through the broken gaps,
Another life dwells

Like a foolish prostitute,
How about outsider literature?

It is the gaze of shattered insensitivity,
There will be no deeply silence than that

# Compensation

Easily,

Let the dream falls asleep in the sea of punishment

   in exil

Because it doesn't have any specific material

   for the subject

---- To avoid yearning ----

Difficultly, I stepped backward the land of illusions

------ To embed the burning ecstasy of the soul,

     into the transparent flesh's sun that knows

     sorrow -------

# LOVE

I have known you blooming as a lotus flower,

Through long nights,
Crying alone, the owl guarding the sacred fire,
The island of water droplets embracing
   the light-year rocks

Such longing,
Such thirst,

I have known the green affection

# Time Gone By

I long for the pain and freedom of the time gone by,
When my unburdened mind felt tragedy,
    without any notions,
Perhaps, it was during those moments
    when I lived my happiest,
Unaware, it slipped away, leaving behind its emptiness,
Even the insignificance of a life as boundless as
    a nomad's journey,
I yearn for
Though I held the essence of my spirit
    within the poorest myself
The desolate sound of the desert's sandstorms,
    the unendurable,
Even those I find myself longing for in nostalgia
The beauty and pain of life,
Even the secrets that age me,
Now, I yearn for the wretchedness of that time
    as well
I yearn for the time I devoted myself to stars,
    seas, clouds, and realms of such freedom,
No, I yearn for the times when I indulged in
    the power of invisible love

# Youth

To possess a somewhat unfading, unique self,
And thus, exude a constant atmosphere
  in any season
The breath of the soul, kindling a small bonfire,
Indeed, that freedom's shore, that tranquil love,
The compensation of truth embedded in poetry,
  the price of purity, the pain!
Oh, youth!
Rest here for a moment,
Let your spirit rest upon this field,
For the lonely tortoise,
For the tiny fish of our hearts,
Like the flame wick of a candlelight,
Flying over the abyss of emptiness,
The innocent faces of children
Beyond the triviality of everyday life,
To remember that laughter,
Lay down in your paradise for a while
Let your bird roll in the sunlight,
Anything at all,
Love!
Freedom!

In that place of dreaming,
Let them stay like peace

# Deformity

## I

Without possessing anything, having nothing
Is that called happiness?

Shall I be sucked into the show-window
Of a black comedy with a puzzled look?
Why?
Just for fun

Shall I go up to the place where the top of the
    skyscraper's sky is visible?
Um···
Warm coffee will stir up my feeligs in the raindrops

The key to enter the bedroom of a new kingdom
Is buried in a pile of fallen leaves
    in the underground cathedral

You're pushing the old gate,
Lying on a dull grayish-brown horizon
For a long time···

The pale moonlight was burning

    the fluttering naked body

For a long time⋯


However,

The back of the compatriots was not visible,

And the symbols and types on the bulletin board

    were not shown

Is it a sin?

Or a grace?

## II

Looking for two candlesticks,

I feel like I should weep a little,

But I rummage through my desolate secret chamber,

But not showing

"As if you were,

The controlled flattering the tongue was beaten

    by the fragments of the times."

"Oh, No!"

Although,

The light green mirage of Bach is not dancing

Please don't shake your terrible butt

Once again,

The tragedy of an era of forced adultery,

Behind the horror of being beaten consciousness,

As if sootheing,

Listen to the sound of God's raindrops

Now, I feel like I should weep

Yes

Let's weep!

# III

Suddenly,
As a pure creature
Never knowing the language of humans,
Rolling around in the sun

Chasing the pecking pigeons,
Sitting on a bench,
In the time of the present and future,
I was pulling a loose arrow

I will dress Ja with brown skin,
In orange and lime colored hi-fashion
I will give her a lemon
I will take her to a tropical island far away,
Where she won't need to ask about history
I was sneakly glancing the spring water in her eyes
Burning incense at the altar of God
In the middle of the sea,
The fragment of her soul from her flesh
   was flying away

To anywhere out of the world

Like fluffy cloud flowers,

Into the clear and warm atmosphere


Pulling the arrow as a backlash from the past


If, in one day (1985), you can't earn 5000 won

   even after working 10 hours,

If you work like a dog and can only get dog food,

If there is no shield to block bullets

For exhausted and dream-deprived isolated soldiers,

The superficial, relative, burgeois,

   No concept of time of Ja

So, even if be ridiculed and mocked,

Lie down for a long time,

In the serenity of the wind and the sun

# The Surplus Humanbeing's Repentance

"She is engulfed in the jaded decrepitude
　　of a third-rate bourgeoisie
With her abundant knowledge and emotions
　　that can not be subdue,
　　due to a frenzied fervor,
　　she has passed by the primal skin of life
She is trapped in antibiotics,
　　dozing in the swamp of language"


"Ah, making me live the solitude
　　that stands at the end,
Forever like a solitary conch shell entwined,
Plunging into the depths of the abyss,
So that there can be no more despair,
So that there can be no more escape,
Toward the fruit that is riped within it,
Igniting like alcohol,
Burning forever,
Living such abundance like a pleasure,
Like a butterfly that gnaws and lives on Logos,
The growing pleasure,
Into the light state of emptiness"

# November

Swept in, receding tidal wave

Even the thought of my love

You made me ache

Now, nothing is shared together

Even the scenery of the senses whining

The abyss of the universe where nothing took root

What remains for me

Is just the empty nothingness of the deep death

   nestled in the afterimage of the apparitions

The light is holding its breath

Look into my eyes,

After leaving somewhere alone,

In such a hollow emptiness,

Even though everything was discontinuity

I trusted you before


The logic of eternal love imbued in a gentle universe,

Also, the breath of God imbued in the universe

Well,

Now, another god called "I" and

The other one, "I", another self-assertive,

Where will I practice separating from the "self"

If I even stay awake through this night

# Reason for Writing


I


With tiny letters,

I want to give my love

To the creations of the Creator,

To all living beings in nature,

Now, even to the fading and vanished forms

    that must be erased from memory,

I want to give my love

I hope to love them for a long time


Isn't life?

Nothing but love,

Beyond loving, is there anything else?

I, giving you my love,

You giving us your love,

We giving this world our love,

The universe giving its Creator love,

And the creations of the Creator


I believe my love will cover the universe, the sea,

Until my soul disappears,

In countless layers of time,

In friction,

I believe it will be immortal

## II

I want to enter the world of countless typesetting

   to love

In there, I want to build a home of love

   for those I love

With a warm flame,

    I want to melt their coldness and comfort them

Sending the breath of my love,

Driving away the loneliness and pain of the universe

Confronting the silence and inhuman sensations,

In the reflective spiral of a vacuum tube,

To give nature's sounds of wind, rain, sun, and dew,

Until the "us" become one in their poverty,

I dream and

Gently place my small hand

On your tired shoulder, powerless,

Until you stand up again

# Towards the Sphere

In the solitary place,
Amidst the lingering loneliness,
That yearning for you,
So I can embrace you generously,
The whispering that separates the darkness and light
  of the sphere

Gently,
Waving like ripples,
Emerging in the breeze,
Reviving
The life of grace

As darkness descends,
One, two, ⋯
Igniting
The altar's candles,
Within that gaze,
In there,
One can truly exist

Part 2

# Infinite Orbit

# Sea

## I

The ever-changing sea always presents itself
   with genuine dignity,
Driving the fresh breeze to raise the scent of the sea
   on the water's surface,
It approaches closely as an affectionate embrace of
   warm love, with kindness and reprimands,
In times of sadness, a comforting sea
    where one can lean and weep endlessly
That love could encompass and cover everything
Harmony of love that can be in sync
Now, just with a single glance,
    the essence of goodness can be felt,
    like an electric current flowing
With the disappearance of the light of goodness,
    life becomes sufficiently futile,
Like an ebbing tide of sorrow over losing a comrade,
The sea moves forward towards
    justice and  camaraderie on Earth,
Toward the sharing and hope of love for all
Until his sought of humanism and the sharing of light

unites us all as one

## II

Through the long passage of time,

Step by step, it has approached,

Revealing its will of existence little by little,

Like the rough hands of a farmer,

Without pretense or adornment,

Always showing its vast expanse of insides

Deep in its heart,

The humble sea resounds!


Today, once again, I seek its freedom

# Loneliness

Many nights, many moments at dawn,
the instant of awakening

With the wind and rain and dew,
In the ever-changing earth,
Within the desolately moistened red soil,
In the river that seems reborn,
My soul always
Such a vast whirlwind of air, like thirst,
Always carrying it within me

Thus, always,
In my soul, intertwined
With the mysterious rustle of trees,
In that abstract sentiment,
In the indescribable
Pure nature's essence,
I breathe in your divine breath,
And it becomes love,
It becomes light,
Blending with darkness,
Giving birth to a new life

# Swamp and Rain

Making the sounds of rushing waves,
    surrendering to the fierce gusts of wind,
Strong raindrops falling on the street
Is living a selective immersion into a new world,
  a cleaning of tedious habits and conflicts?
  like a breakup of worn-out people
  who don't want to live together any more,

Love is simple, naive  and vague,
Boldly,
Indifferent foolishness
In fact, the essence of love exists only
  in the recognition of the subjective self,
Like the association of sounds of rushing waves,
  the crashing sounds of strong raindrops
  in the desperate situation
Is living an experiment in infinite patience
  during moments of Unbearable living?
The weariness of making non-existence exist
How can we endure?
Helplessness in the face of this seemingly endless,
  monotonous, tyranny of time

# A Stormy Hill

Within the soul's flame of a black hole,

It begins to pull him in,

Merging with a single dance,

Blending into his soul,

Flowing with the immortality of a phoenix,

Continuing with the flow of one's blood

# Absence

In the midst of the absence of love,
Even if I try to hold onto the gaze of that love,
In the midst of memories,
I believed I could live with the presence of poetry

"Like a severed filament of a light bulb, I am lonely,"
Hemingway's soliloquy,
Embodies the pain of losing the light of life

Losing body temperature in the inserted coldness,
Even without the concrete presence of love,
Without metaphors,
Enveloped in strange, unfamiliar, and dull objects,
Like a religion,
Like a philosophy,
I believed I could live with the presence of poetry

# Scar

Compelled to talk, but as if caught in aphasia,
The heart doesn't lift the latch

Darkness and life, blue···
A long extinction that must be accepted
    as a part of life, the tears of blood
The soul did not make a sound

The bright karma with silver halo!

Beyond the secret chamber,
Even the abyss can't find the coar
    that escaped from me
The Microcosm of Cold Stars
The wind of the origin

The soul was the love
Embracing only the deep and blue tranquillity
    of indifinite scenery of the self

And,
Love was the soul

# Genesis of the Soul

Oh, soul without fleeting dreams!

Oh dewdrop!

Nourished by the leaves of emptiness,

By the breath of the divine,

Return to the homeland of the night,

To the life of cold stars,

And be restored

Into eternal rest

# Grand Canyon

When we fearlessly rush forward
Towards the vast plains of life spread out
   like a great river
To start life anew,
The fossilized dinosaurs, like child,
Revive with the sap of life,
With warm blood,
They returned the hope of poverty,
The happiness that was slipping away

Even in the long winter cave,
When overcoming the battle scars
   with the predestined mystery and demons's faults,
Even when unhappiness erases laughter in the eyes,
The life of love and innocence,
The sun, rain, and wind,
Miraculously preserved the fragments of consciousness
Even in the extreme weakness

# Unity of Self and Nature

A tree clings to the steeply carved cliffs,
  exposing its roots,
A desperate sight for survival
It reaffirms the ordinary principle
  that life aims to exist

As if sucked into the clouds
  from the edge of the cliff,
Toward the sky and atmosphere,
Several trees stand flutterly

With the sky, clouds, and wind,
I want to fly into that scenery,
  to become one point with it

With the sea, trees, sky, and clouds,
Atmosphere and wind,
When I stand before them,
I,
I forget myself and become one with the nature

# Blank Paper

In front of a blank paper,
  I began to wrestle with despair
Fear and lethargy are wrapped in scars
    like a defeated soldier
The profound simplicity of complete emptiness was
    like a mirror reflecting
Everything as it is, allowing things to pass through,
    like the black Olhue's mirror
Recalling the compassion of Rimbaugh,
    stained with wounds
Recommending his youthful espri
    as he broke his pen,
I, too, must break my pen
    in the self-destruction of a hidden poem,
In the face of the paradox
    that I have to lose everything
To choose a resignation
    that has no choice but to resist
For what, forward what, for nothing,
Until it becomes a sediment
    that's coming out of me one day
Can I wait for poem?

When I am weary of waiting and can't do anything

about the degenerated nature

How will I cope with the empathy I cannot let go of?

Should I seek compensation for everything

I must let go of while waiting for him?

In the void where nothing can be achieved

# BAN

On the last night, tiredness weighed heavily,
I couldn't hear the sound of rain
  as I sank into a deep sleep,
In the morning, the bright atmosphere outside
  was already past the sunrise,
I knew I woke up later than usual,
Only after pushing aside the curtains
  in the living room
Seeing the wet pavement streets,
I realize that it had rained all night,
Also, there was no journey tossed and turned
  by memories
Like an insubstantial person,
In the long ellipsis of an irresistible feeling
  of psychic inevitability invoked in the bed
If the experiment on the essence of love is
  as enticing as the smell of freshly baked bread,
  maybe get the peaceful happiness
But it resembles the damage of psychological
  madness that drains our strength,
Just like a movie protagonist accustomed to
  getting hurt,

Eventually becoming familiar with the dissolution

   response to wounds,

Like an aestheticist unhesitating

Subordinating everything to transcendent telepathy

   beyond time and space,

Even though his eyes have sunk deeply,

   contemplating salvation through destruction

It being the entire existence at the tyranny of

   one point in life,

Thinking of the healing and oblivion mechanisms

   of time,

I realize that when this crazy love drama reaches

   its extreme,

It will extinguish itself somewhere along the way,

And even the remnants of that spark should be

   sent away with the wind

# For Love

To love you was to experience the union of your
  soul and mind with the physical embrace, the
  essence of life itself
Night became the richest joy of impoverished love,
  dreaming of union as you transcend space and
  time, flowing as one in humble existence
Your soul filled my body like air and caress my soul,
  I surrender to the sublime pinnacle of love
Tonight, once again, beyond oceans and mountains,
  your lullaby seeps into my moonlit bedroom,
Our souls will diffuse, soaring into the mystery of
  this night, to the boundless sea, the sky, and the
  enchanted forest

# Freedom

Oh, King of Peace, come among us!
Grant us the communal life
    where we can unite with each other
Through your mercy and love

Lord, keep us from living in the hell of self-doubt
And hatred without the unity of love
Help us overcome the mundane nature
    that your love teaches us to conquer
Lord, lead me with your mercy and unite me
With your Spirit of love to set me free

My Lord, God!
You have given me body and soul, nurturing me
Amidst countless conflicts and sins,
Have compassion on me and cleanse me
    with your mercy
Only you can lead me to live in true truth
    and experience true freedom
Lord, unite me with your Spirit

# Intoxication of Flame

I have not yet found your language,

Like a paper tiger that slips through among people

Granting your territory,

It can save the sad one-dimensional froth of life

In the scenery of days cast away and dried,

It brings a little tipsy of a flame

What can be repercussion?

The reincarnation of the mask!

What could give rise to it

To touch the cosmic realm of the brow?

Sacred and mournful breath!

# Gone By

Even though I call you "who are you",
You may not understand
The subtlety of the connections
Like the dry leaves on the field,
Primarily,
Amidst the overflowing dry coughs,
In the human forest,
You will not truly see the sorrowful gaze

## Beatrice!

Oh, eternal companion of my heart!

On a rainy, melancholic morning,
  impoverished poet Doobo
How much I adore that pathetic Doobo?

In the profound sorrow of emptiness,
In the heavy abyss of solitude's descent,

Returning to the bending trees in the rough rain,
I long to collapse in this rain-soaked morning

I wish not to utter a single word,
Into the hollow self, into the pinnacle of empty life,
If only I could,
Immersed in the pure realm of intuition
  where language does not disturb

Yearning to exist like philosophy,
Sensing delicately from the tips of my cells,
Shall I act upon the desire to plunge into that
  rough rain this morning, or not?

The rain calls me, but why does my soul tremble

    only within this barricaded city?


How happy I once was with that rain and the trees,

The fields and that rough rain,

    my old companions calling me

This morning, beyond the maze-like continent's junction,

Can I break free from the moss of time,

    from the inertia, to reach them?


Your collective hypnosis and collective

    unconsciousness lie deep in that forest


This morning, I wish I could banish

    even the appropriate language from my brain,

    if I could


In the direct intuition of truth,

Returning to that original purity,

I want to exist as myself


Beatrice!

Eternal romanticist!

Ultimately,
It is a matter of enjoying freedom

Religion begins with the abandonment of language,
As the entryway to absolute freedom(?)

True freedom is the liberation of true self,
The process of becoming one
   with myself, the world, and God,
A return to absolute purity

Thus, the body and mind of the Saint are filled with it,
And there, only love exists

When free, the soul is filled with love

## Sawee Dance

When you choose to live like that,
Within yourself, you alienate the tangible "you"
   from the intangible "you"
Always feeling like something is slipping away,
The swaying of true things,
The momentary stillness of dense eternity,
In the fleeting instant that time escapes,
Through the dance of emptiness,
The dance of no action, in the truth
You return to reveal your true self
That is the true manifestation of you

# Rain Falls

"Rain falls, and in its descent,

It beckons us to glimpse

   the essence of our primal existence,

    if only for a moment, into the silence

Within the tapestry of nature,

    woven with senses and intuition,

It leads us into the realm of divine freedom

Life's beauty lies in its transience,

Flowers bloom exquisitely

    as they journey towards their zenith,

Within life's core resides

    both emptiness and genuine liberation

Our memories of love shimmer within layers of time,

And the very act of living for that love

    renders life boundless

The moments shared between you and I,

    within the fabric of time and space,

Etch the memories of love

A day will come when we return,

But our soul will longer than reincarnation

Let's go! Let's go!

To that expanse of sky,

To that expanse of air,

To that expanse of universe"

# kitten kiri

Today,
My kitty climbed over the fence,
Sneaked into the neighbor's house again
But, nothing is fun,
Elderly court!

She has been dozing off all day long?
The grandma!

Who will caress you?

Sleeping on mom's lap would be nice

After lunch,

Sure!

Let's take a short nap!

# Embracing Solitude and Loneliness

The solitude and loneliness I used to enjoy
Now cast away in the hustle and bustle of daily life,
Fading into regression like a withering habit
But when they are forgotten and longed for,
I yearn to immerse myself
  in deep solitude and loneliness,
Loneliness becomes a vegetal essence, a scent of
  thick vegetation and grass leaves'photosynthesis,
Which is ingrained in vegetative people
It feels transparent with the bitter leaf juice and the
bitterness of light green tea at the tip of my tongue

However, solitude is like a decrepitude body
  by the exhaustion from hard labor
Nobody care for, abandoned by love
  that is forgotten and lost,
In a broken heart with no more waiting,
The sad eyes of a soul devoid of intelligence
A mold that spreads in the wall of despair
  endured alone,
With the virus penetration,
  there's nothing more to struggle with

It's like a crumpled piece of paper,
   like flesh cling to every bone joint

"Why is the pain?" asking

Within Baudelaire's intoxicated eyes,
   seems to represent everything with extreme spirit
Solitude drives out language,
   and intuition and emptiness go beyond it
Through solitude and loneliness,
   I hope to truly purify and become transparent,
As if returning to a religious ritual,
Regaining an exalted, profound human consciousness,
But before the pain of existential solitude,
It appears merely an extravagant gesture
   in the face of alienation and suffering···

# Swimming

In order to be free,
I release myself into the water

As I stand on the edge of ancient memories,
Recalling the moments when I learned to flap
    the wings of free will,
The momentary unease and loneliness,
Returning to the absolute freedom
That already, cannot be free innate
The azure expanse of the sky,
The unity of the absolute goodness
Already, in the plaintive traces of the tired fins
I recall the fleeting nostalgia that has passed by

# Happening

Love has not yet crossed my doorstep,

But I think about its end

For now, it's just a simple curiosity,

A trivial happening

With a funny wrinkle in his eyes that bursts into

   endless laughter


From the clothes that a person who never knew

   how to express pain, if hurt even once, takes off,

Rise the night sea's tidal wave

Does only God know him?


Love is the desire for ultimate unity

So what should I do about it?


Happening is merely a happening, after all···

# Margins

The days I have lived were different from
    the methodology of loving you,
So with the wings of youthful aspirations,
I couldn't get close to you
But the transparency of the sheer margins of
    past days,
In the heart of the first frosty earth,
    seeds for eternity were conceived,
And the prelude of love was sprinkld on the festival
    of fragrant flowers,
For the reproduction of noble life

# Annual Ring

Gazing at you without any preconception,

To embrace you within me,

To know you deeply

And carefully,

I begin to whisper,

Having seen your annual ring

# Infinite Orbit

It was fine to be blocked in front of a dead-end wall
As if already compensated behind resignation,
Tilting the last glass of the isolated things
that can only be overcome by transcending,
God returns nonchalantly
Like the collapse behind belief,
Turning it into nothingness

Exhausted to the extreme,
A Big Bang of bones and blood,
Rising into the infinite orbit as a cosmic supernova
Perpetual life embedded in the unknown 4th dimension,
Replicated memories embedded in unbreakable atoms
In the light of that magnetic force,
An outsider is drawn in!
The sea of rebirth urges
The return to the cosmic space,
Calling out to me

# Endless Rush

At the end, like a Möbius strip catching its own tail,
Breaking free from the contours of living,
At the dead-end cliffs of pursuit,
Even if driven into the membrane of hemisphere
    on range,
A discontinuous morning, difficult to escape the
    temptation of ceaseless conspiracy,

The multiplication of time

Poor god!

Now, a farewell longing to discuss drugs and alcohol,
···Requiem···
···Grave···

Time's multiplication will clothe
The familiarity of a conspiracy

Each note of the poem
Throws the soul into the sea,

The spirit of agnosticism

Dances fully on the walls,

The end of accepting me!

I

Finally

Begin to evaporate

# Small Boat

As always,

Standing at the edge of the sea,

Immersed in the traces of a long history,

With transparent emerald waves,

And a dazzling horizon beyond the sky's blue,

Fixing my gaze on a small boat

That vanishes into a single point,

Sailing alone into the sun, sky, and wind

   of the South Pacific,

Immersed in the eternal mystery of profound silence,

I imbue the love of life,

Soaked in the humidity of long breath, flying away

Like a light-hearted soul

   with frail and expansive wings,

Riding the wind,

Towards the end of questioning,

To the temple of the lone awakened love,

I lift myself onto the small boat,

Seeking the love that remains

# Epitaph

I am glad to have lived on
  this dazzlingly beautiful Earth,
Embracing nature in all its colors
    of red, yellow, and green,
Earth, the blue star shining with a blue halo,
A person who lived loving life, overflowing with love

Anywhere there was trees, I was content,
Warmth from the sun made me never feel lonely,
With just the fresh ocean breeze, I could exist,
Even just,with the scent of loess soil, I could be one

A person!

Having known, felt, and loved nature,
A person who was happy,

Laid to rest here

# Absolute Freedom

I wish the keyboard could capture the inspiration
  of the initial struggle
But I can't catch the wind that's disappearing
  in a moment
Feeling you in the realm of God
  was a momentary nirvana
It was the breeze that touched your existence
  in the absolute purity of the great nature

# Swaying Blade of Grass

Engaged in the tug-of-war

between love and frivolous emotions,

Like a vainly swaying blade of grass,

If love were to ride the currents within

　　the gravitation of the immense galaxy of love,

Even a love that feels it might die from being apart

And Even if it starts to escape from my grasp

　　like the wind,

Even if none of it truly belongs to me,

Life's flow continues, autonomously,

Returning once more to a serene me

Part 3

# Elements

# Elements

......

......

......

Even so, in my youthful days,

Already, through implicit sharing,

Embracing the emptiness of life wholeheartedly,

With the scorching Algerian sun and wind,

    the elements

Within them,

I no longer ask for anything more,

Pledging to remain like them,

Transforming into an element,

Embracing true freedom,

In that emptiness

I search for the true existence,

Enveloped in genuine freedom,

Amidst the absurdity that made us weep helplessly,

And from the world that was chewed up

    like crispy sand for a moment

Toward our true homeland,

To the love we willingly accepted upon

  awakening from slumber,

To that camaraderie,

To the homeland of the spirit we'd go back to,

I pull out the unfeigned existence

# Flesh

Printing out an entire lifetime with the single element
    called "love",
Filling one's solitude with snowflakes,
Dreaming of a real paradise,
For the wounded soul,
Eternally and absolutely free in its own dance,
Breathing only within its own peace and unique light,
But weary and yearning for the its true essence!
Unwilling to accept anything impure beyond oneself,
In a mind solidified with the horn of a unicon
Where even the sweet songs of charming birds,
And the melodies of dew-drenched leaves
    and wildflowers,
Overflowing with longing and abundance,
Exist solely as their own pages within me,
Even for the long legs over the fence
    who need the daily bread of love
For those who living with his anger on his chest,
No different from Jony with dementia,
Only exist as a the reaction of inertia,
Even fester with wounds,
Forgetting the God who sacrified his flesh to people

As if removing the mechanism of eternal love,

   always and forever

For the invisable you,

For the other God,

A small universe questioning the law of love,

As much as the words he writes, he is "me"

"I" am the one with invisable wings,

Reflected through the honest flesh of love


---If God permit that I accepted God's love,

   God dedicated his holy flesh to love humans

   If then, I learned to abandon and kill myself,

   would I be liberated and find my true self? ---

# I Know the Way to the Sea

Like a hidden secret,
The sea, my heart's entirety,
At the end point of life,
The sea I must reach in the end
Once I arrive there,
Life will merge with my soul and spirit,
Filling me with complete divine love,
The place where life's end leads to eternity,
Where the ranks of existence extend

You, who exist with the same soul as mine,
Becoming one with the same consciousness of freedom,
As the subject of existence,
Into eternal nothingness, eternal being,
Now, we'll be together forever

I know the way to the sea

You, who have learned from long scars and tragedies,

When this dream is erased,
Now, I must return to

You, my true home

Therefore,

I know the way to the sea

----- The sensation of evolving spiritual life,

Enveloped in the miraculous joy of light,

Adorned with destiny and mystery,

The heart of this fleeting universe

Into the sea of the soul ------

# A Tear Jar

While thinking of God,

I have always been crying

Amid the awe of life,

While contemplating the square of life,

Once again, like that,

Always,

I was crying

# My Lord, God!

Allow me,
To be captivated by Your beauty,
And let me offer
Incense in adoration and praises,
At the sacred altar of worship

# Alone

In consciousness,
There exists an unapproachable sorrow,
Like a wound,
Refusing to be shared,
Rejecting any healing
It desires to go alone

In the selfishness of a crafty civilization
Sad self-portraits painted with cultural logic

Without compromising
To the hypocrisy and the materialistic vulgarity

Towards the place of love,
As an inaccessible sorrow,

Let's go alone

# Bea!

No matter how intoxicated I become,
There is something still lacking
It is the enchantment of beauty,
It Feeds and wets my soul
So, I call it "the love of God",
God would willingly offer everything for us
    who came as a human

God is the ultimate beauty

He liberates me,
In the indulgence of sublimation,
Making life in emptiness in truth

My Lord, God!

For You,
In every moment of this life, You have given me,
For You,
Grant me a life that can be returned

# Heathcliff

"I cannot forgive her
    for leaving me behind and dying"
"I will pray to God,
To make her restless and wandering,
Until I die"
"May her soul become a ghost,
    haunting around me…"
"I cannot live in a world without her"

Upon hearing of Cathy's death,
Heathcliff, banging his head against a tree,
Howls like a beast in despair
Heathcliff's obsessive love
Keeps Cathy's spirit as a ghost on the stormy moor

Love is not something anyone can do
Love is a matter of the soul
Without going mad, no one can truly love

# Fragrance

The feast of fragrance for my beautiful love
　fades away,
And the longing scatters the remnants
　of the last scent in the breeze
On the day the stars fall from the sky,
The female poets' fishes become even deeper blue,
And the reason I loved you
Is to make everything in your eyes shine like jewels,
The reason I loved you is the light in your eyes
The reason I loved you
Is that everything within you turns into precious gems

Now,
I leave behind you
Just for a while,
But you will always be
The origin and the end of me
Nevertheless,
Even for a short while,
Goodbye!

# Nature

Like this,
With a lost heart,
I cannot feel you
With frozen senses

I try to restore the warmth of my heart,

With the remnants of love,
I restore my DNA

Countless thin
Arrangements of bases
Scratched
Under the sap
Life loses its soul
Confined in spacetime

I want to feel you
To express my love to you
But I can't even move
Facial muscles

The heart is always tired
In search of its homeland
And always has been away

# Ghost

Shall we contemplate?

Life demands precise logic
No, I crave precise and logical reasoning

Why do I wander like a ghost?

Like a ghost,
Without knowing where to go

Yet,
Smiling faintly as if knowing,
But still,
The logic hasn't been established
In fact, one side of the brain is lazy,
Resisting reasoning
No straightforward, clear explanation

Do you want to know?

Life is bland
Is it harsh and bitter to you?

Days are many,

Think beyond tomorrow, in the distance⋯

Why am I,

Wandering in this life like a ghost?

Why do consciousness and soul have

so many rooms?

Living as if forgotten,

Yet, always love remains,

In my soul keeps the flame

# Emigration

Becoming accustomed and familiar

The most fearful thing is the sense of loss

Leaving behind what was familiar,

Having to let go of what was tamed,

Like a lost child, venturing into a new world,

Inevitably pushed away by the unknown,

Fear and discomfort

The mind can't anchor,

The history of emigration is not all cheerful

Entering the maze as if untangling a thread,

Losing and discarding things,

Pursuing and going after something,

The framework buried from the beginning,

without any origin,

A bit of melancholy,

like a spoonful of cream in coffee,

Stops under the sun,

A bending of fate that melts away,

The world⋯

But from the distance of an ocean,

The true essence of the sense of loss,

Unknown and yet so keenly felt,

Longing for the time when that paradise

Will embrace the heart and return the soul

So, for several years and seasons,

Me and my child,

No one,

No touch, that land,

Protecting endangered nature and life,

In that paradise,

Yearning for the time when our kitten kiri kiri will

    find psychological stability and attachment,

Our hearts and souls,

In the free air, with the leisureliness of everyday life,

From the flawless purity of nature,

Being suntanned and solidified

    by the Pacific Ocean and the sun,

Filled with the winds of the ocean

......

It remains folded there, like a stationary page

Once again, it must be continued,

In the pure nature,

Meeting the delicate lives,

That sense of happiness, that excitement,

Crossing the day and beyond···

# Georba

Venturing out to the sea,

Under the transparent sun,

Dancing with the wind and the atmosphere

Finally, as if becoming a Greek Georba,

At last, becoming the flesh and bones of an
   unexcluded life

Dreaming with the light of ecstasy

Into the realm of absolute freedom,

Believed to be possessed only by gods

# Distant Dawn

Throughout the night,

With my whole being,

With my entire heart,

I await you

Engulfed in the nightmares of sorcery and magic,

Implanted by the darkness of chaos,

In the ruthless and cruel war of vulgar species,

Never

Progressing further,

Even amidst reason

And artificial intelligence

Rendered stagnant,

There is but one passage

Holding all of this in suspension,

On the path towards you,

"The distant dawn breaks."

# Part 4

# Nourishment of the Heart

# In the Midst of Life

Life is devoid of words, what can I say?
In the middle of the desert,
    embracing the frigid night like inky darkness,
With only a constellation of distant stars
    reminiscent of my homeland,
I am not lonely,
    even if stripped of all but the pilgrim's dance

Since the day of broken devices
    and severed communications,
Unable to return to yesterday's mundane routine,
I have faced the morning
    with the broadness of the hopeful sun,
Amidst fears and the growing thirst,
    listening only to hallucinations' echoes

Yet, amidst these extreme situations,
    I've endured the recoil of continued extremities,
Replacing life with meditative contemplation
    through the power of the mind

Such is life

_ _ _ _ Vivaldi, his most convincing music shines

　through the brilliance of a free spirit

　and genius of spirituality

　Inspiration, complete concentration,

　His melodies embody that _ _ _ _


Life is such,

Like Kahlil Gibran's poem states:


"Life is a lonely island adrift in the vast sea.

Yet, on your island, on my island,

　no one can reach."


"No matter how deep your darkness,

The lantern of your neighbor cannot illuminate it."


Ultimately, life is something to endure alone


I must labor

To survive, I must pretend to stumble

　in the labor market for a while

Living is about creating and choosing

   the responsibilities for myself,

Embracing those responsibilities like a cog

   in the wheel of fate,

We cannot stop it from rolling


I must labor and seem to forget myself

   for the time being

To return to myself, I must wait for Labor Day

   to end and enter the Sabbath

Until then, consciousness enters a state of rest


Always,

The wind blows,

And I, who prefer lying down, search for the long

   daylight chair of the sabbatical year,

There will be no better place than a field of grass

   and sunlight rays alone


Living by embracing oneself,

Living is like that

Having my beautiful baby, the beautiful nature, music,

The human intellect that can steal glances,

Living well even in solitude

Like the Alpine girl Heidi,

Living simply and purely like a fairy tale

However,

I cannot let go of my lingering attachment to love

The vague expectation and dream about love,

    perhaps it is the person's body temperature

Love is like a rest that only the person's

    temperature and scent can provide

So now, I revise my dream of love

I now want to discover that

    person's temperature and scent

To love someone and obtain someone

To love when finding and discovering that love,

With all my heart,

It's still not too late

To find that unknown love…

To become happy,

I must find true love

Finding my perfect companion

Working, seeking love, cherishing my baby,

That's how our life passes

Thomas Merton defined

The soul as intelligence and love

We wish to see our souls

Beautiful soul,

Guardians of the realm of the soul,

If love does not mix blood and flesh

   to carry it to the soul,

It is worthless

But,

Can we truly love purely?

Only love remains to fly infinitely to the soul

# Arrow Prayer

Can we experience the power of arrow prayer?

Do you believe in the sacred ability of prayer

without doubt?

It's not about expecting miracles


Entrust yourself to the power of prayer,

Give everything to Him,

Let's go!

Yes

Alone, like the horn of a unicorn, let's go


Let's pray more frequently, more often

I will have more time to love God


Every time I pray, I am captivated by His beauty

Through prayer, God purifies our souls

And leads us to his mysteries

God is not far away,

He is within me, through the path of my soul


In order to experience God and feel His beauty,

I must cherish each and every moment of prayer

## Common Goodness

Even in the moments
   when I couldn't wait any longer,
I waited for you as an courtesy of love
   for a long time
A corner of my heart,
Perhaps, started forgetting you
When I grew tired of waiting
   while thinking about propriety

As love began to embrace propriety,
I had already started moving away from you,
Beginning to free myself from attachment

The moments I wished for unity with you
   to fill my life
Seemed too long,
And the time I blindly yearned to see you
Seemed as if life existed for that purpose alone

Now I have erased you from my heart,
But I am grateful to you
You will have to live diligently, as that is my share

The price of our lives becoming irrelevant
　　to each other
Will be for your happiness,
And I pray that God's mercy and grace
　　will always be with you

"Love is based on your happiness."
The distance of love always existed
　　as a rational spirit between us,
Just like your unwavering faith
Love was always rational

I hope you become a great light of spirituality
That wipes away many people's tears

Perhaps, the reason we couldn't be together
　　was because of that,
So I want to call it "common goodness"
I always believed that the common goodness
　　should take precedence over individual happiness

# The Unbearable Lightness of Being

With the unbearable lightness of existence,
It feels as if one could reach a warm sea
  hidden somewhere,
Finally finding solace in the completeness
  of a hometown from long illusion, weary
  emotions of deception, and exhaustion
It's as if the essence of a just cause,
Poetry, politics, movies, an open society,
A future society we yearn for,
The social cause of all of us, a single thread,
  form of all that is allow us to live?
Does the true unknown outer sustain the emptiness
  of a despairing, self-centered human?
What keeps us going?

The unbearable lightness of existence,
Does the social bond spur me?
Does society keep me alive?
While always preparing to escape from it,
Why, society also binds us to social causes?

An economy with a human face!

Standing with a human face,

  like the most cynical materialistic desire···

What kind of rationality is

    the task we need to solve that deceives me?


Dreams are something to share?

If I'm alone in this world I'am already in a mess

To the most unsociable human being

It's still in the realm of interest to bond the most

Are you restraining me?

# Relative Love

Relative love is comfortable,

Rational love avoids absolute wounds

Love is not just about possessing you,

Merely expanding your boundaries

    in the name of freedom

Does not truly grant freedom

Laughable is the belief that freedom is seen

    as rebellion against norms

To genuinely love a partner, it must start with

    acknowledging their freedom,

Those who think they have reached the state of

    true love by granting complete freedom

Can give up if they lack confidence

    No, it's disgusting


Is love pretending to be free?

Is it a fight for ownership, unable to let go?

Is love merely eros?

Should only spiritual, platonic love be respected

    as love?

Is love among men and women a selfish,

    carnal desire?

What matters is that love is

the expansion of the heart,

A mental process of combining halves to form

a complete entity

It's like an endless yearning for a beloved partner,

It's a combination of loved one and your soul

It's an unbearable lightness of being

That cannot endure without merging

Not turning black like a charcoal briquette

Due to possessiveness,

But unbearable lightness of existence,

A dream of love like an unattainable yearning,

Your soul cuddling your lover's soul

The energy of love entering your lover's body,

Becoming one with their entire being

Through the power of love

# Bubbles

Too much flood of speech about hot issue
   is like a bubble
The reason I always want to remain silent
   amidst the flood of overflowing words
Is that I don't want to add more to
   what has already been said
I want to perceive and understand
   phenomena and things in the world
From an emotional approach,
   from the essence of life
Always overwhelmed by too many words,
Trying to feel and comprehend them emotionally,
That is my primal and most essential way
   of dealing with things and people
Approaching and perceiving things with emotions,
Understanding them with the resonance of the heart
   and the feeling of the soul,
That is my way of encountering the world

From the moment I let go of words,
My heart is filled with the gentleness of internal
   spirit, the light, and atmosphere of love

Thus, silence seems like a pathway

  to becoming complete

Through the light of goodness


Why does God remain silent?

Why does He always empty us?

That is God's way of love

Silence is His way of love


To become complete,

I want to bend alone like fog in a deep mountain

The trees are just there,

And the shaking is indistinguishable

  between you and me


What Zen question and answer is this?

Who are you, the Zen master?

Just go in and meditate deeply

To the very bottom of the universe's abyss

Splash Splash Splash!

# Nourishment of the Heart

Today, once again, I couldn't find it
The nourishment for my heart…
I have been hungry for a long time
But no matter where I looked,
I couldn't find solace for my heart

Where are the whistling birds of summer?
Where have all the great masters
    of the mind hidden?
I need you like bread
I need "The Seeds of Contemplation"
    — by Thomas Merton —

The great masters I once loved
    are no longer by myside
I have to endure this alone
Learning to love life

Young!
Your illusions cannot offer anything
Isn't God's grace something like this?

Knowing one's own essence

Realizing God's grace


Ignatius of Loyola!

I happened to encounter this great spirituality


When the soul is tormented,

And you want to transcend to a dimension

    of divine faith,

Gazing at things with a loving and gentle eye,

But then returning to meditation,

After contemplating the truth and beauty of God

    with the light of reason,

And after forming the habit of insuppressible prayer,

I realized that I must enter through contemplation

# Secret!

To those who seek to escape from the pain of life,

Is religion akin to a drug?


Various illnesses,

Various pains,


Why is there suffering?


When in agony, look to Jesus Christ!


Hanging on the cross, groaning in severe pain,

Jesus with nails in his hands and feet,

His side pierced, and water flowing out,

His head covered in blood from the crown of thorns,

Mockery, ridicule, and scorn surrounding him,


Such an incapable Son of God,


Jesus seemingly abandoned even by the Almighty

God, whom he is part of,


Completely alone, as if abandoned by everything,

Where is the kingdom of Jesus?


We, who were like followers of other religions,

Accept and serve the God of Israel

Because He is all-powerful and existed before the

    creation of heaven and earth,

And because He has called us to the kingdom of love,

He desires to be praised alone


"We pray to be merciful to us,

Deliver us from hardship and persecution,

Free us from this irrational world."


"The enemies always plot against us,

Conspiring to bow us down before their idols

Lord!

Break them with your shield, spear, and sword,

Save us from their ridicule and mockery,

And on the judgment day,

May the heavens and the seas encircle the whole earth

As your shield."

If what we do does not return to God,

If it does not align with God's will,

We will not receive blessings from God

Do you seek miracles?

Do you hope for magic?

Believe and seek,

Experience miracles

He will give to you

He will give abundantly

In the Old Testament,

_____ Success in life depends on God's blessing,

How can one receive God's blessing, the blessing of
the firstborn, so that the descendants are filled with
blessings to the brim?

How can one obtain God's blessings?

According to the Bible,

"My beginning was humble,
    but my future will be grand"

"Whoever believes in me believes in the one
    who sent me and accepts that person"

"First, seek His kingdom and His righteousness"

"Unless you become like a little child,
    you will never  enter the kingdom of heaven"

"Father, may they all be one"

"I am leaving you,
    but I am sending the Holy Spirit to you,
Do not be anxious or afraid"

"I will be with you until the end of the world"

"I am giving you peace

The peace I give is different from

 the peace of the world,

Do not be anxious or afraid"


Therefore, if Christ, the triune God, resides in us,

The kingdom of heaven is within us


Embrace the Lord Jesus Christ, our Savior,

And believe, then you will receive blessings

# Creation

A person who sought freedom

from all materialism, falsehood, and idols,

A person who rode the pure stream of a solitary life,

gazing at the transparent dawn on the earth

from her solitude,

A person who truly wanted to live as herself

Simon de Beauvoir!,

A person I wanted to follow

like a guiding star and respect,

Her unwavering self-awareness and unyielding

commitment, to a life of conviction

Shone like a faint ray of light,

Showing me a way

out of my confusion and wandering,

She traversed the between the celestial

and mundane, manifesting the path of moderation,

reenacting life,

I aspired to make her way

of living my life's standard

And thus, she became the great victor who affirmed

my life, a life that basked in the beauty

and brilliance of the shining sun,

She was truly a sincere and honest philosopher,

  breaking free from the society's values and

  morals, tainted with conventions and prejudices,

She sought to realize the true existential value

  of a woman as an individual human,

For her, the ultimate value of existence was living

  as her true self

Hence, she didn't conform to the passive role

  of a woman, following traditional virtues,

  indoctrinated and imposed on her

Instead, she actively engaged in her life, participating

  in and investing herself in contemporary life with

  her subjective values and capabilities

Her approach was expressed

  through creative endeavors,

  breaking away from the conceptual worldview

And critically embracing the conditions

  and circumstances of existence,

By actively engaging and participating in the society

And the world she belonged to, she vividly

  demonstrated how one should live  and struggle,

  as shown in her writings

For her, it was not about conforming

to the irrational and unconscious traditions

as a traditional woman

But discovering herself and shaping an active life

through rational intellect and resolute

consciousness, rejecting existing ideas and values

not validated by her reason

It was a philosophical agony for her,

embodying the truth of existentialism,

a life towards freedom guided by reason,

It enlightened me

The greatest strength and support for her,

which could have been her guiding light and

anchor, were the encouragement and support

of her great philosophical companion,

_ Jean Paul Sartre _

# Zen

To execute your existence fully with your own body,
To be fully awake in every moment,
Even in the seemingly trivial acts,
Without the need for any special consciousness,
To concentrate your entirety
That is what they called the practice of Buddhism

Always, if only I could,
I want to hold myself there, where the breath lingers,

But I always leave me and drift away

# The Sabbath

No excuses are allowed

Perhaps what I love the most is God

Can one be liberated from the guilt of not going to
    church while claiming to love God the most?

Simonae Bayou, what was the reason
    she didn't go to church?

Was it because of the majority of
    non baptized people?

No, it was because of her philosophical truth
    and objective study

For example, because there were original myths
    similar to the creation myth that she couldn't
    accept, even in other religions

But above all, I admire her poor soul that lived the
    most virtuous life

Her poor soul dedicated to understanding seems to
    speak for herself in every moment

Devoting each moment to philosophical
    contemplation and understanding,

Living according to her conscience,
    and pursuing the truth

In our lives, it's difficult to actualize every moment

with the realization of our thoughts

It's too difficult to execute the will to dedicate

oneself to what one believes is right,

With all one's spare energy

Her soul was a figure demanded by Korean women

In dark times

Who will take responsibility for the conscience

of the times?

Who will devote themselves for humanism?

We needed such intellect and soul desperately

at one point in time

No, we still need them forever

Now, we have come out of a long tunnel

But we still seek the lighthouse's light to protect

the times

The path we must take still stretches endlessly

before us

If I hadn't met God,

I, as a human being, would have been in a long and

boring place without love,

Unable to find any glimmer of hope

It would have been a world similar to Helen Keller's

Screaming in the darkness,

A desperate situation, where one doesn't know

   the miraculous prism of nature bathed

    in pure light, untouched by reason


God is love

That love is salvation

Many hope to meet this oasis


If I hadn't met God,

If I couldn't realize the God

  who is the source of beauty like that,

My life would have had no hope

God is hope


However,

Though God is like air, God is like breathing,

However,

Please allow me to be alone on the Sabbath

Even being able to love you would be a lie

Because love is an allocation of my time and effort,

It requires pouring myself out

Love requires giving myself

But I did not allocate myself to you

I cannot speak of love


Furthermore, love is to take away all fears

Love is God's promise to be with us

    until the end of the world

Just like God's love,

Our love should stay by the side of the beloved,

Devoting ourselves with all our hearts

    and sincerity to love


It means turning oneself into nothingness

# The Beginning of Love

Love is soothing someone else's wounds
It should start from loving others

There is no human who can be free
    from psychological trauma
Sometimes, the wounds we want to erase
    from our memories
Should be buried in the depths of the sea,
   where even memories cannot find them
Never dig them out
Never let a psychiatrist or a shaman blow them away

Those wounds will heal themselves someday,
With more time, experiences, and wisdom
    in the future
Until they can heal themselves,
Let's forget them
After all, life must go on

"Where can you find a soul without scars?"
_Arthur Rimbaud_

Sometimes, living itself is like hell

It is a punishment that we must endure this hell